MIDDLEMARCH

Middlemarch

Epigraphs and Mirrors

Adam Roberts

OpenBook
Publishers

https://www.openbookpublishers.com

© 2021 Adam Roberts

ISBN Paperback: 9781800641587
ISBN Hardback: 9781800641594
ISBN Digital (PDF): 9781800641600
ISBN Digital ebook (epub): 9781800641617
ISBN Digital ebook (mobi): 9781800641624
ISBN XML: 9781800641631
DOI: 10.11647/OBP.0249

Cover image: Vilhelm Hammershoi, *Interior with a Mirror* (1907). https://commons.wikimedia.org/wiki/File:Vilhelm_Hammersh%C3%B8i_-_Interior_with_a_mirror_(ca.1907).jpg. Cover design: Anna Gatti.

Contents

Introduction

This short book aims to turn a modest, one might even think trivial, literary labour into something more substantial, going beyond one particular novel into broader questions of novel-writing, character and narrative. My starting point is tracking down those allusions and quotations in *Middlemarch* that have hitherto gone unidentified by scholars. Most of these quotations are located in the chapter epigraphs that George Eliot provides throughout, citing other writers or confecting her own pastiche blank verse or prose. Unpacking these epigraphs as well as the other quotations, and exploring their relationship to the body of the text, frames or grounds a broader discussion of the novel. It seems to me that these epigraphs, taken as a distinctive part of a larger network of quotations and allusions in the text, contain important resonances for the way Eliot's novels generate their meanings. For, indeed, the way the novel as such generates its meaning.

It may be that my opening paragraph comes across as defensive. We wouldn't want that. It was Eliot's practice in all her novels to add epigraphs to her chapters, some quoted from and identified as by particular authors, others created by herself in the style of a poet or an 'Old Play'. She was by no means the first author to do this, of course; popularised by Walter Scott, it is a practice that goes back into the eighteenth-century. It could be argued that the textual practice of heading a chapter with a short quoted text apes the practice of the popular sermon, just as the related habit of larding the novelistic text with quotations apes a conversational practice that does the same thing, one widespread enough that it could itself be satirised—by Scott, and others—as a mode of pretentious pedantry indicative of a lack of imagination, or even of an overcompensation for discursive unconfidence. Abel 'Dominie' Sampson in Scott's second novel *Guy*

 https://doi.org/10.11647/OBP.0249.06

Mannering (1815)—one of the most popular individuals from Scott's vast gallery of characters—is a key figure here. Sampson is a man 'of low birth', whose capacity for learning was encouraged by parents (who hoped 'that their bairn, as they expressed it, "might wag his pow in a pulpit yet"') prepared to scrimp and save to secure their son's education. But he proves too shy and awkward to be a preacher—a 'tall, ungainly figure, [with] taciturn and grave manners, and some grotesque habits of swinging his limbs and screwing his visage while reciting his task', he ends up as tutor in Godfrey Bertram's stately home, Ellangowan. The point is that there is something simultaneous creditable *and* ridiculous in Sampson's learning, laughed at as he is by his fellow university students:

> Half the youthful mob of 'the yards' used to assemble regularly to see Dominie Sampson (for he had already attained that honourable title) descend the stairs from the Greek class, with his lexicon under his arm, his long misshapen legs sprawling abroad, and keeping awkward time to the play of his immense shoulder-blades, as they raised and depressed the loose and threadbare black coat which was his constant and only wear. When he spoke, the efforts of the professor (professor of divinity though he was) were totally inadequate to restrain the inextinguishable laughter of the students, and sometimes even to repress his own. The long, sallow visage, the goggle eyes, the huge under-jaw, which appeared not to open and shut by an act of volition, but to be dropped and hoisted up again by some complicated machinery within the inner man, the harsh and dissonant voice—all added fresh subject for mirth to the torn cloak and shattered shoe, which have afforded legitimate subjects of raillery against the poor scholar from Juvenal's time downward.[1]

We're at the other end of the scale, here, from Thomas Hardy's *Jude the Obscure*, and not only because Scott styles his character as a comic rather than a tragic figure. Jude's learning proves useless to his life, where Sampson at least finds a social niche as an (admittedly overqualified) tutor. His speech is a mixture of simple Scots idioms and learned allusions, his, as we would say nowadays, catchphrase 'Prodigious!' and various Latin tags: 'as he shut the door, could not help muttering the *varium et mutabile* of Virgil'.[2] Scott, with nice irony, sometimes uses these

---

1   Walter Scott, *Guy Mannering, or the Astrologer* (Boston: Estes and Lauriat, 1893), ch. 2, https://www.gutenberg.org/files/5999/5999-h/5999-h.htm
2   Ibid., ch. 15.

as markers of Sampson's educational *limitations*, as when, encountering Meg Merrilies unexpectedly in Edinburgh he reveals his superstitious primitivism: '"Get thee behind me!" said the alarmed Dominie. "Avoid ye! *Conjuro te, scelestissima, nequissima, spurcissima, iniquissima atque miserrima, conjuro te*!!!"' Meg, with less book-learning, has more common-sense: '"Is the carl daft," she said. "What in the name of Sathan are ye feared for, wi' your French gibberish, that would make a dog sick?"'[3]

Scott's next novel, *The Antiquary* (1816), tackles this same business of the allusiveness of discourse from the other side of social hierarchy. Jonathan Oldbuck, gentleman-antiquarian, embodies an obsession with the textual and material past, at once fussy and gullible. His speech is larded with Latin and he orients himself in all respects with reference to a notional past. Scott is laughing with rather than laughing at (but laughing nonetheless) when he has Oldbuck seek to reassure the unlettered beggar Edie Ochiltree: 'don't suppose I think the worse of you for your profession [...] you remember what old Tully says in his oration, *pro Archia poeta*, concerning one of your confraternity—*quis nostrum tam animo agresti ac duro fuit—ut—ut*—I forget the Latin'.[4] The point of these allusions is not that we the reader should recognise them, nor even that we should chase them up (of William Lovel, also present, and also a gentleman, Scott notes that these words reach his ears 'but without conveying any precise idea to his mind'). Rather the point is that, by their very opaqueness, they signify to us the character's comical pedantry, as well as his blindness to his own ridiculousness. They are a kind of phatic articulation of dead learning rather than an invitation to recontextualise the passage in which they occur.[5]

Perhaps we readers and critics of Eliot ought to treat the epigraphs and allusions in *Middlemarch*, and her other novels, in a similar manner;

---

3   Ibid., ch. 17.

4   Walter Scott, *The Antiquary* (Boston: Estes and Lauriat, 1893), ch. 4, https://www.gutenberg.org/files/7005/7005-h/7005-h.htm

5   It is perhaps fitting that I use a footnote to identify a third means by which Scott adds specific allusion to his texts, beyond chapter epigraphs and characters quoting old authorities—footnotes themselves, a mode Eliot herself very rarely deploys. There have been several studies of the influence of Scott on Eliot, most often concentrating on her more manifestly 'historical' writing: see for instance Andrew Sanders, *The Victorian Historical Novel 1840–1880* (London: Palgrave Macmillan, 1979), Harry E. Shaw, *Narrating Reality: Austen, Scott, Eliot* (Ithaca: Cornell University Press, 1999) and Miriam Elizabeth Burstein, *Narrating Women's History in Britain, 1770–1902* (Aldershot, Hampshire: Ashgate, 2004).

that is to say, as meta-indicators rather than as Ariadnean threads to follow, or miniature windows to peer through. The content of the various quotations and allusions are always clear enough, and there is always a comprehensible relationship between what the epigraph says and the content of the chapter it heads-up. Perhaps I out myself as merely a Sampson or an Oldbuck by refusing to let things go at that. Of course we make an exception for the editor of a scholarly edition of the novel; she would, amongst her many textual duties, be expected to look into such things. But for a regular reader, or a critic with an eye on the larger significations of the novel, to get bogged down in such minutiae looks, surely, like a misapplication of energy, as liable only to clog and impede the larger flow.

Clearly, given the book I have here written, I don't believe so. On the contrary, it is my argument that exploring these various allusions and epigraphs *un*impedes the rich flow of significations the novel generates— that these potsherd texts-within-the-text are keys that unlock new rooms or, to shift metaphors (and in doing so to anticipate the larger thesis of this book) mirrors that refract back upon our experience the textual vistas opening to us. Such a claim can only be evidenced by the actual work this study undertakes, and perhaps you will conclude by the end that such a claim stands unsupported. I must, at the very least, concede that the joy a scholar finds in exploring these questions may strike a less Casaubonic individual as both arid and—which is worse, in this context—atomising, disconnecting, a key to no mythologies.

That, though, is precisely the point. In her earlier novels, as in her later, Eliot weaves her text out of descriptive prose, dialogue, observations from life, data from her research, literary allusion, quotation and often obscure epigraphs. In *this* novel she does all that and also includes a character for whom abstruse allusion and obscure epigraphs are his life's passion. This situates *Middlemarch* as, amongst many other things, a novel *about* epigraphy, about identifying and deciphering quotation and allusion, as well as a novel *constituted by* those things.

There is a related question to do with, precisely, obscurity. When Scott's Oldbuck quotes a bit of Cicero so abstruse even *he*, it turns out, can't remember it, we're on safe ground reading the allusion in terms of its inaccessibility. But when Eliot cites, indirectly or otherwise, Sappho and Pascal, Homer and Lucretius, perhaps the intertexts are offered in the tacit belief that readers will recognise and understand without the need of a prompt from an editorial footnote. Perhaps Eliot assumes an audience sufficiently au fait with their own reading as to be able to walk with her, hand in hand, through her own richly informed allusiveness. This seems unlikely, and not only because Eliot's own reading was capacious beyond most people's. Still, it may be. I'm reminded of Virginia Woolf's first broadcast by the BBC—on 29 April 1937, as part of a series called 'Words Fail Me', the only recording of her voice to have survived—in which she observed:

> Words, English words, are full of echoes, of memories, of associations—naturally. They have been out and about, on people's lips, in their houses, in the streets, in the fields, for so many centuries. And that is one of the chief difficulties in writing them today—that they are so stored with meanings, with memories, that they have contracted so many famous marriages. The splendid word 'incarnadine', for example—who can use it without remembering also 'multitudinous seas'?[6]

Though we are, I think, entitled to wonder what kind of person drops words like 'incarnadine' into everyday speech, Woolf's point is a sound one. Some allusions tap into a common reservoir of collective reference and understanding. That context used to include much of Shakespeare, the more famous English poets and even a fair bit of Latin. For most of Eliot's first readers, in the 1870s it also included Scott. Nowadays a reduced set of Shakespeare quotations might still function as common cultural currency, together with a wider range of references to film and pop-music.[7]

---

6   Fiona Macdonald, 'The Only Surviving Recording of Virginia Woolf', *BBC Culture* (28 March 2016), https://www.bbc.com/culture/article/20160324-the-only-surviving-recording-of-virginia-woolf

7   Howard Erskine-Hill makes a related point with respect to epigraphs: 'In a little noted epigraph Pope quotes an ancient authority as saying that poetry is no obstacle to entering into the wider world. But today an inscription of verse, or indeed prose, at the head of a wider work may seem an impediment, rather than an incitement to read on. Where learned or foreign languages are used what was once a spur has become a clog. The impatient eye glances over the bit of Latin (as it may be) with the reflection: "Oh, yes, a Latin tag; that was the old practice". The time is past when a writer might quote *quantum mutatus ab illo* and expect the reader to recognise the author, the work, the speaker and the situation'. 'Pope's Epigraphic Practice', *The Review of English Studies*, 62.254 (2011), 261–74 (p. 261), https://doi.org/10.1093/res/hgq027. The Latin—taken from *Aeneid* 2:274–5—makes his point for him.

So, yes: there are a number of ways we, as readers and critics, might 'take' an allusion or epigraph in a novel like *Middlemarch*. Since such items have, without wishing to sound merely utilitarian, a textual *function*, it is only courtesy to the reader that this function is still operable in the instance that said reader is not Casaubon. 'It is tactful', as William Empson once wrote, 'when making obscure references, to arrange that they shall be intelligible even when the reference is not understood'. He gives an example, from a lesser-known poem by Marvell ('The brotherless Heliades/Melt in such amber tears as these'), and adds:

> If you have forgotten, as I had myself, who their brother was, and look it up, the poetry will scarcely seem more beautiful: such of the myth as is wanted is implied.[8]

This is fair enough, and certainly describes Eliot's way with quotation and epigraph. But Empson goes on:

> But something has happened after you have looked up the Heliades; the couplet has been justified. Marvell has claimed to make a classical reference and it has turned out to be all right. This is of importance, because it was only because you had faith in Marvell's classical references that you felt as you did, that this mode of admiring nature seemed witty, sensitive and cultured.

This is a deeper point, and one equally applicable to Eliot. Her extraordinary learning—all the more extraordinary given that so much of it was autodidactic—stands as a kind of pledge to her allusive textual praxis. We believe her, and when a mini-Casaubon such as myself burrows into the specifics, what we uncover, without (I think) exception, shows that our faith is justified. Christopher Ricks, quoting this passage from Empson, adds that a text 'without being dependent on our knowing certain things, yet may benefit greatly from our doing so'.[9] That's a very to-the-point statement of one of the rationales of the present study.

To separate out chapter epigraphs from 'allusion and quotation' more broadly is to touch on a slightly different question. For one thing, the question of 'weight' enters the frame. Theodore J. Ziolkowski recalls that

---

8   Empson, *Seven Types of Ambiguity*, rev. edn (New York: New Directions, 1947), pp. 167–68.

9   Christopher Ricks, *Allusion to the Poets* (London: Oxford University Press, 2002), p. 2.

In the original typescript for *The Waste Land* T. S. Eliot cited a passage from Joseph Conrad's *Heart of Darkness*—the one ending 'The horror! the horror!'—because he found it 'much the most appropriate' and 'somewhat elucidative.' But when his mentor, Ezra Pound, doubted that Conrad was 'weighty enough,' Eliot omitted those words and chose instead the more ostentatious quotation, in Latin and Greek, from Petronius's *Satyricon* that now adorns the title page. In her anthology, *The Art of the Epigraph*, Rosemary Ahern cites over two hundred further examples, mostly but not exclusively from fiction in English.[10]

I've never really understood why Ezra Pound and T. S. Eliot believed the ludic decadence of Petronius's *Satyricon* counted as 'weightier' than Joseph Conrad's diamond-hard articulation of existential despair. Although, in saying so, I suppose I'm being a little obtuse: Pound's point is specific not to this particular text but to the larger cultural idiom. Classical literature trumps a novella published only a few decades earlier simply by virtue of its ancientness. George Eliot is not immune to this bias, such that we may intuit that for her an epigraph from an 'Old Play' outweighs one from a newer drama. It implies, at least *in potentia*, a deep-time three-dimensionality that offsets and so adds perspective and richness to the more historically specific and limited—1829–32—story being told.

The illusion of depth is part of the function of epigraphs and allusions. This is a separate matter from the more commonly perceived work of epigraphs 'to mark an aim, or strike a keynote', as Howard Erskine-Hill puts it.[11] There are other contexts to the tracing of unidentified quotations than pure Casaubonism, and there are other ways of conceptualising what an epigraph is. For example, we might take it as the text from which specific chapters develop a core idea, as a sermon expands homiletically upon a Biblical text—a Dorothean, rather than a Casaubonic way of treating them. Then again, we might see an epigraph as something tiny that contains, when magnified, beautiful or important microscopiana—a Lydgatean perspective. These three perspectives are not proposed merely to be facetious. Since *Middlemarch*, as a novel, remains one of the great fictional portraits of barren scholarly pedantry, and given the dangers a study such as this present one runs in trudging

---

10   Theodore J. Ziolkowski, 'The Craft(iness) of Epigraphs', *The Princeton University Library Chronicle*, 76.3 (2015), 519–20, https://doi.org/10.25290/prinunivlibrchro.76.3.0519

11   'Pope's Epigraphic Practice', 261.

a similar dry-as-dusty path, it is important to keep in mind that, for Eliot, a quotation could be something other than an iteration of abstruse learning. To remember that it could be a germ. A seed.

More recent Eliot scholars who have explored this question have, by and large, generally thought so too. But it didn't used to be that way. David Leon Higdon's fine essay 'George Eliot and the Art of Epigraphs' argues that 'the epigraphs form a continuous commentary defining and shaping the chapters. They are foreshadowing what follows, and to some degree shape, control, and condition the reader's reaction to the chapter'.[12] But he also notes how rarely (this, in 1970) Eliot's epigraphs have been considered by critics at all, and quotes a couple of negativities of judgement:

> Only Henry James and J. R. Tye have considered the epigraphs in terms of conscious artistry. James dismisses them as 'a want of tact,' and Tye concentrates on the epigraphs George Eliot wrote herself. Although he concludes that they frequently make 'an illuminating adjunct to the text of her novels,' he appears mildly irritated with her for using them at all and dismisses them somewhat hastily. If in fact the epigraphs are decorative, they may be dismissed as a literary counterpart to the 'gingerbread' of Victorian architecture.[13]

I do not, any more than does Higdon, consider Eliot's epigraphs 'gingerbread', although I'm also attempting here something rather different to his reading of epigraphs and main text in terms of 'organic form'.[14] It is a larger argument than can be fully accommodated here, but 'organic' seems to me exactly the wrong word to apply to an art form as consciously worked, as mannered and textual, as the novel; and doubly unfitting when applied to what are (by and large) some intricately meta-textual and intratextual patternings. If we take 'organic' as a synonym for 'functionally intrinsic' or 'non-arbitrary' or something along those lines, then it would describe better what's happening in Eliot's art

---

12   David Leon Higdon, 'George Eliot and the Art of the Epigraph', *Nineteenth-Century Fiction*, 25.2 (1970), 127–51 (p. 131).
13   Ibid., 19–30.
14   'The epigraphs have an organic function in her novels. This theory provides a coherence for the various artistic effects they create individually. Four major tendencies-structural allusion, abstraction, ironic refraction, and metaphoric evaluation—may be delineated. She also uses epigraphs to describe characters, to present a character's unconscious thoughts, and to argue for realistic presentation, but these epigraphs are few in number'. Ibid., 134.

(although these are not, after all, what the word actually means). Then again nobody would accuse Eliot of scattering epigraphs randomly through her fiction. We can, I think, take her artistry as axiomatic. And since my focus is on the way the 'small' text of the epigraph (or quotation) interacts with, illuminates the 'large' text of the chapter (and the novel)—which is to say, the formal relationship between small and large textualities inherent in the mode—I make little distinction between those places where Eliot is quoting somebody else and where she is confecting her own faux-motto or quotation.[15]

I've already quoted from Christopher Ricks' *Allusion to the Poets*, and it is worth touching on another point from that subtle, insightful book. For Ricks, literary allusion is always more than a matter of barren source-hunting—always more than mere scholarship for the sake of scholarship. It is, rather, a question of inheritance. His chapter on William Wordsworth (himself an important writer for Eliot) opens with the question: 'what for Wordsworth is the central or essential inheritance? And how might this validate the inheritance that is allusion?'[16] The same question stands to be answered for Eliot, and her own allusively rich fiction. That *Middlemarch* is centrally about inheritance in a legal and (as we would now say) genetic or hereditary sense is not irrelevant to this question, of course. Indeed the way Eliot's novel negotiates its own multiple textual inheritances, and the way it explores the problematics of (for instance) Dorothea's compromised inheritance from her dead husband, are, I would argue, complexly interwoven one with the other. Going back to the work of unpicking the specifics of allusion and epigraph in the novel is a way of elaborating this matter.

What remains to be seen, I think, is whether these epigraphs, and these myriad embedded nuggets of quotation and allusion in the body of the text, figure predominantly as Casaubonic, Dorothean

---

15   For a contrary view see Michael Peled Ginsburg, who finds a kind of conceptual short-circuit in Eliot's self-authored epigraphs: 'when an author writes his own epigraphs he [*sic*] presents a text (the epigraph) as a text which precedes him and the insights of which his story in some way repeats. At the same time he subverts this assertion because the epigraph is his own. Thus, by creating pseudo-epigraphs the author presents himself as his own origin and himself generates the truth which he later repeats or puts into question'. 'Pseudonym, Epigraphs, and Narrative Voice: *Middlemarch* and the Problem of Authorship', *ELH*, 47.3 (1980), 542–58 (p. 548), https://doi.org/10.2307/2872795

16   Ricks, *Allusion to the Poets*, p. 83

or Lydgateian entities. Of course, were it only the first of these, and neither of the other two, there would be little point in writing this book. But it seems to me that Dorothea's scholarphilia, her sense of herself as defined not by the quotidian logic of the other people in her ambit but by her connection with learning and theology of the past—the ground of her attraction to Casaubon—is a humanising[17] of Casaubon's drier, more cerebral passion for epigraphy and quotation. What lifts the novel, the stroke of structuring genius that makes *Middlemarch* so marvellous a piece of writing, is the way Eliot balances this world against Lydgate's approach. For him the natural world is a text to be interpreted in the light of science, rather than literature, mythography or religion. It is true that Eliot traces the diminution in his ambition from achieving significant medical breakthroughs, to a society doctor 'alternating, according to the season, between London and a Continental bathing-place' who has done nothing more to advance medical science than written a treatise on gout ('a disease which has a good deal of wealth on its side', as the narrator waspily notes), this shrinkage is neither an altogether reprehensible, nor a textually irrelevant, business. We are first introduced to Lydgate as a 'scientist' as someone interested in the very small, and the very small is wholly the tenor of Eliot's type of realism. Epigraphs are small, but they bear close attention, not in terms of Casaubonic pedantry but in terms of Lydgatean microscopy. So although the novel's final chapter records that Lydgate 'always regarded himself as a failure' since 'he had not done what he once meant to do', we as readers might wish to console him that he at least showed the way. The paragraph from which I've just been quoting concludes with the novel's last mention of Lydgate, that

> [his] temper never became faultless, and to the last occasionally let slip a bitter speech which was more memorable than the signs he made of his repentance. He once called [Rosamond] his basil plant; and when she asked for an explanation, said that basil was a plant which had flourished wonderfully on a murdered man's brains. Rosamond had a placid but strong answer to such speeches. Why then had he chosen her? It was a

---

17 Indeed, though we are perhaps disinclined to accept that this is also part of Dorothea's reasons for marrying her first husband, we can also read it as an eroticisation.

pity he had not had Mrs. Ladislaw, whom he was always praising and placing above her. And thus the conversation ended with the advantage on Rosamond's side.[18]

This is elegantly oblique, the closest the novel comes to conceding what many readers, surely, have thought—that Dorothea and Lydgate ought to be together. That, in other words, there are two ways in which Lydgate 'had not done what he once meant to': the way of scientific research and the way of finding a mate worthy of him, as he of her. This is more than merely romantic daydreaming, since Eliot reverts the disconnection back upon Dorothea, whose yearning for a husband with a great mind was misdirected towards a man whose mind was in thrall to a dead past, rather than a man whose mind was open to the exciting possibilities of a scientific future. As between these two options Eliot brings-in a third—Ladislaw's politics—but although *Middlemarch* is fascinated by the 'realism' of scholarship and by the 'realism' of science, it has little to say, actually, about the 'realism' of politics (unlike, let us say, *Felix Holt*). This is not to say that party politics is irrelevant to either the novel's plot or its design; but that myth and science are two modes Eliot finds more eloquent for articulating her theme.[19]

I am going to argue, in this study, that Eliot's epigraphs are, textually speaking, kinds of glasswork, like the lenses and mirrors that render a microscope or a telescope operable. By looking with them and through them, we see greater detail and greater scope in Eliot's novel. Mirrors are a way in which we 'look back', and this is a novel deeply fascinated by 'looking back', as engagement with tradition, as scholarship, as tracing inheritance and also as regret. And in another sense mirrors (and lenses) facilitate the work of science, and the work of science is also the work of realism. Or to be a little more precise, what distinguishes

---

18 George Eliot, *Middlemarch* (Edinburgh: William Blackwood and Sons, 1871), 'Finale', http://www.gutenberg.org/files/145/145-h/145-h.htm

19 On the novel's use of science, see in particular Michael York Mason, '*Middlemarch* and Science: Problems of Life and Mind', *The Review of English Studies*, 22.86 (1971), 151–69, https://doi.org/10.1093/res/xxii.86.151; Sally Shuttleworth, *George Eliot and Nineteenth-Century Science. The Make-Believe of a Beginning* (Cambridge: Cambridge University Press, 1984); Lawrence Rothfield, *Vital Signs: Medical Realism in Nineteenth-Century Fiction* (Princeton: Princeton University Press, 1994). On religion in the novel, see T. R. Wright, '*Middlemarch* as a Religious Novel, or Life without God', in *Images of Belief in Literature*, ed. by David Jasper (London: The Macmillan Press 1984), pp. 138–52.

Eliot's humanist realism from the kinds of *le naturalisme* being practised on the Continent, is her resolution to balance the scientific (microscopic, or telescopic) observation of the world with the literary, mythic and spiritual apprehension of the same object. The differences between Eliot and a writer like Émile Zola are instructive in this context. Zola also grounds his realism in a particular iteration of a medical-scientific idiom:

> To the second edition of his first major novel, *Thérèse Raquin*, Émile Zola added a famous preface in which he sought to make his intentions clear against accusations of immorality: 'my objective was first and foremost a scientific one. I simply carried out on two living bodies the same analytical examination that surgeons perform on corpses'. To those who claimed he had an unhealthy interest in moral and human decay, he retorted that he had become 'engrossed in human rottenness, only in the same way as a doctor lecturing to students about disease'. These medical images persist right through his accounts of his own work; over twenty-five years later, he would say of *Doctor Pascal* (1893), the last volume of his epic Rougon-Macquart novel sequence, 'it is a scientific work, the logical deduction and conclusion of all my preceding novels', adding that his aim has always been '*to show all so that all may be cured*'. The protagonist of that novel, Dr Pascal, is clearly modelled on Zola himself, from his obsessive tracing of the Rougon and Macquart families' genetic inheritance to his passionate relationship in middle age with a much younger woman. Doctors play pivotal—and generally positive—roles in *A Love Story* (1878), *Nana* (1880), *Pot Luck* (1882), *The Bright Side of Life* (1884), *The Earth* (1887), and *The Debacle* (1892). When Zola publishes his collection of essays arguing for Naturalism, his title *The Experimental Novel* (1880) refers not to artistic but to medical experiments.[20]

But despite writing a doctor as a major character, Eliot's approach in *Middlemarch* is considerably less surgical than this. She does not want to cut open or eviscerate, but she does want to observe, to gather and to sift data, and that's the kind of physician Lydgate is. The microscopic focus is fitting, the epigraphs and quotations appended to this great novel are mirrors, and can be read as mirrors, and can shine lights on Eliot's achievement.

To those who think it strange to construe Eliot's realism through epigraphs and quotations, rather than through (say) the accumulation

---

20   Dan Rebellato, 'Sightlines: Foucault and Naturalist Theatre', in *Foucault's Theatres*, ed. by Tony Fisher and Kélina Gotman (Manchester: Manchester University Press, 2019), pp. 147–59 (p. 148), https://doi.org/10.7765/9781526132079.00020

of pseudo-documentary representations of aspects of life as it is lived,[21] I could make the perhaps over-obvious rebuttal—that for Casaubon, epigraphs *are* his lived experience—in order to expand upon it. After all, our lives are not some string of purely-accessed pearls of Dasein, or are not *only* that. Our lives are also not only determined but to an extent constructed by the texts we read and remember, the plays we have seen, the poems we have read. Wisdom is lived, but also mnemonised as proverbs and quotations. Any strategy of literary realism that did not include quotation and epigraphy would be jejune.

We might say that books (like *Middlemarch*) are texts, whereas human beings are texts only by analogy. But several of the epigraphs of *Middlemarch* return to the idea of people *as* books. The first chapter of Book 2, 'Old and Young', begins with an Eliotic pastiche, a snatch of dialogue from an ersatz Elizabethan or Jacobean play:

> *1st Gent.* How class your man?—as better than the most,
>   Or, seeming better, worse beneath that cloak?
>   As saint or knave, pilgrim or hypocrite?
>
> *2d Gent.* Nay, tell me how you class your wealth of books
>   The drifted relics of all time. As well
>   Sort them at once by size and livery:
>   Vellum, tall copies, and the common calf
>   Will hardly cover more diversity
>   Than all your labels cunningly devised
>   To class your unread authors.

There's something odd about this epigraph. On its face, it seems straightforward. The First Gentleman poses an important question: how do we judge human beings? Indeed this is, arguably, the key question, for Shakespeare who returns to the disjunction between seeming and being over and over ('there's no art to find the mind's construction in the face' and so on)—and of course for Eliot too. But Eliot's phrasing in this confected epigraph is strangely ambiguous between 'how do you

---

21 There has been a good deal of scholarship that has taken this approach of course. See for instance Anna Theresa Kitchel, ed., *Quarry for Middlemarch* (Riverside: University of California Press, 1950); Lilian R. Furst, 'Not So Long Ago: Historical Allusion in Realist Fiction', in *Through the Lens of the Reader: Explorations of European Narrative* (Albany: State University of New York Press, 1992), pp. 133–48; Kate Flint, 'The Materiality of *Middlemarch*', in *Middlemarch in the Twenty-First Century*, ed. by Karen Chase (Oxford: Oxford University Press, 2006), pp. 65–86.

judge men in general?' and 'what is your judgment with respect to *this* specific man?' 'He' dresses in fine clothes, but does his character match his outward array? When rephrased that way the answer is obvious: of course not. It would be as ridiculous, as the Second Gentleman says, in words that glance at the old proverb about not judging books by covers, to arrange one's library by size, or binding. Different books bound in the same kind of covers will of course contain many different kinds of content. Indeed, it's an observation so facile that it must send us back to the original epigraph. Is that all it's saying? Well, no. For one thing, there is the—strange, surely—styling of books in a library as 'the drifted relics of all time'. Not living things, brought alive with every reader, but inert fossils. A 'relic' is something left behind, something we have left behind: the Latin *reliquiae*, 'remains, relics', is from *relinquō*, 'I leave behind, abandon, relinquish'. Books are here relinquished as texts with which to engage—'unread authors'—whilst simultaneously being assembled, collected, sorted into library shelves. When we think of it like that, the point of the epigraph shifts ground. It becomes not about how we 'read' people (indeed, it is very specifically about how we don't 'read' people), but instead how we dispose of them after we have 'collected' them.

What kind of person 'collects' other people? It speaks, perhaps, to a particular, objectionable kind of character: the sort of person who assembles friends and acquaintances not for the sake of those relationships, or out of genuine interest or affection, but because those friends and acquaintances are (perhaps) famous, wealthy, or aristocratic, as social adornments or for their social utility rather than as people. Whether we would necessarily call such a person a hypocrite (although they might, of course, be a hypocrite) is uncertain. But perhaps their 'problem' is rather the reverse of this, a too bald acceptance of the conventions of society on their own terms, a position pharisaical rather than common-garden hypocritical perhaps. This is because Eliot is using this epigraph to set-up the first meeting of Lydgate and Bulstrode, and therefore to foreshadow the banker's eventual fall. It is Bulstrode, in this exchange, who seems better but is worse beneath his cloak.

> The banker's speech was fluent, but it was also copious, and he used up an appreciable amount of time in brief meditative pauses. Do not imagine his sickly aspect to have been of the yellow, black-haired sort: he had a pale blond skin, thin grey-besprinkled brown hair, light-grey eyes, and a large forehead. Loud men called his subdued tone

an undertone, and sometimes implied that it was inconsistent with openness; though there seems to be no reason why a loud man should not be given to concealment of anything except his own voice, unless it can be shown that Holy Writ has placed the seat of candour in the lungs. Mr. Bulstrode had also a deferential bending attitude in listening, and an apparently fixed attentiveness in his eyes which made those persons who thought themselves worth hearing infer that he was seeking the utmost improvement from their discourse. Others, who expected to make no great figure, disliked this kind of moral lantern turned on them [...] Mr. Bulstrode's close attention was not agreeable to the publicans and sinners in Middlemarch; it was attributed by some to his being a Pharisee, and by others to his being Evangelical. Less superficial reasoners among them wished to know who his father and grandfather were, observing that five-and-twenty years ago nobody had ever heard of a Bulstrode in Middlemarch. To his present visitor, Lydgate, the scrutinizing look was a matter of indifference: he simply formed an unfavorable opinion of the banker's constitution, and concluded that he had an eager inward life with little enjoyment of tangible things.[22]

Lydgate, immune to the moral lantern, makes a judgement based on medical ('the banker's constitution') rather than social or conventional grounds. Nonetheless his assessment is not so far removed from that of wider Middlemarch opinion. Bulstrode performs acts of charity, and collects friendships—'"I shall be exceedingly obliged if you will look in on me here occasionally, Mr. Lydgate," the banker observed, after a brief pause'—not for their own sake but for the lustre they cast upon his reputation. He does not enjoy the things in themselves, he bolsters his own ego, knowing as he does his own fundamental unworthiness.

The thing is, a doctor is another kind of person who 'collects' or assembles people. Physicians collect patients in order to attend to their health (and in order to earn money) but also less for their own sakes and more as iterations of medical symptoms. The question for such a collection becomes not 'is this person a saint, knave, pilgrim or hypocrite?' but 'what is their pathology and how might I address it?' with, in the case of many doctors, Lydgate included, 'how shall I turn this person into a data-point in my research?' I am the son of two doctors. I know from personal experience the extent to which they observed people, and chatted to one another, in terms of a congeries of potential symptoms. Family journeys by car would be the two adults

---

22   Eliot, *Middlemarch*, ch. 13.

in the front saying things like: 'what about her, by the roundabout? A thyroid complaint, do you think?' 'Hashimoto's disease, perhaps? But what about *him*? Ehlers-Danloss, maybe?' They were, I believe, typical of their profession in this regard.

And, of course, there is a third kind of person who 'collects' people: the novelist, that individual whose friendship is always compromised, to one degree or another, by observational apprehension of real people as a resource for future writing.

The larger point, it's worth drawing out, is that if all of our relationships with other people are as instrumental as this—as denuded as this—then we are not living as full a human life as we could, or should. Such people are living smaller than they should, and are missing the chance to enlarge their lives. It is one of Eliot's great themes, of course: Silas Marner, by limiting his life to gold, endures a pigmy existence; and when he loses his gold and gains Eppie his life enlarges in all the important ways a life can enlarge. I do not suggest the comparison out of mere facetiousness when I say: precisely this step-up from small to large, from suggested-at potential to expansive experiential fulfilment is enacted by the shift from epigraph to actual chapter, and more fully from epigraph to whole novel. The really significant thing is that this dynamic, this small reflection to larger reality, also describes the way we can turn from novels—even great and profoundly insightful novels like *Middlemarch*—to life as it is lived. We do not, or at least (Eliot is saying) should not, live only in books. The idea that art is a kind of mirror is the fundamental of literary mimesis as such. Eliot's mirrors are usually small, and are often coded for narcissism—Rosamond's existential smallness, Eliot implies, is a function of such narcissism. We may use mirrors only to admire ourselves, but equally we may use mirrors for more admirable purposes, and the smallest of Eliot's mirrors is also one of the most revealing, in her beautifully compacted metaphor for the writer's art with which *Adam Bede* opens:

> With a single drop of ink for a mirror, the Egyptian sorcerer undertakes to reveal to any chance comer far-reaching visions of the past. This is what I undertake to do for you, reader. With this drop of ink at the end of my pen, I will show you the roomy workshop of Mr. Jonathan Burge, carpenter and builder, in the village of Hayslope, as it appeared on the eighteenth of June, in the year of our Lord 1799.[23]

---

23   George Eliot, *Adam Bede* (Edinburgh: William Blackwood and Sons, 1859), ch. 1, https://www.gutenberg.org/files/507/507-h/507-h.htm

Indeed, *mirror* and *admirable* are, marvellously enough, versions of the same word (they both descend etymologically from the transitive Latin verb *miror*, 'I am astonished at, marvel at, admire, am amazed at, wonder at').

Mirrors distort of necessity, by giving us a smaller, inverted simulacrum in place of the larger, richer reality; and some mirrors distort—through spotting on their surface, or curves in their shape—more than others. Then again, for some people precisely those distortions are what make mirrors valuable: as (two topics to which I return in the book that follows) telescopes, or microscopes. And if Eliot is quite properly suspicious of distortion in her art, she is not so dogmatic a mimetic artist as not to realise how worthwhile it can be, in the right circumstances. Early in *Middlemarch*, Dorothea believes herself the mere distorting mirror of a world that Casaubon apprehends *in toto*:

> 'He thinks with me,' said Dorothea to herself, 'or rather, he thinks a whole world of which my thought is but a poor twopenny mirror. And his feelings too, his whole experience—what a lake compared with my little pool!'[24]

By the end of the novel, Dorothea's twopenny mirror is, we realise, a better lens—more like Eliot's own drop of mirroring ink—than Casaubon's desiccation. The final gesture of the novel, when it abdicates representation of Dorothea and Ladislaw's life altogether, replaces the representation through a glass, darkly, with a nothingness that allows us to imagine their face-to-face. The epigraph to the chapter in which Dorothea's tuppeny mirror is mentioned is interesting too. It takes its lines from *Paradise Lost*, book 7:

> 'Say, goddess, what ensued, when Raphael,
> The affable archangel . . .
> > > Eve
> The story heard attentive, and was filled
> With admiration, and deep muse, to hear
> Of things so high and strange'.[25]

Admiration again: linked with *muse*. By 'deep muse', John Milton presumably means deep thought, pondering and considering the

---

24 Eliot, *Middlemarch*, ch. 3.
25 Ibid.

angel's words; but we can perhaps take the words, as recontextualised in this novel, at this point, as saying something more. Because it does not stretch matters, although it does entail a rather striking gender inversion from the literary norm, to see Casaubon as Dorothea's muse: as the figure whose idealised form inspires her to her characteristic action, and so imparts motion to the whole of Eliot's story. Milton reoccurs in the novel's next mention of a mirror; this time not Dorothea's tuppeny glass but Casaubon's spoon. Eliot, adopting the narrator's voice, cautions her readers against any 'too hasty judgment' with respect to the old scholar:

> If to Dorothea Mr. Casaubon had been the mere occasion which had set alight the fine inflammable material of her youthful illusions, does it follow that he was fairly represented in the minds of those less impassioned personages who have hitherto delivered their judgments concerning him? I protest against any absolute conclusion, any prejudice derived from Mrs. Cadwallader's contempt for a neighbouring clergyman's alleged greatness of soul, or Sir James Chettam's poor opinion of his rival's legs,—from Mr. Brooke's failure to elicit a companion's ideas, or from Celia's criticism of a middle-aged scholar's personal appearance. I am not sure that the greatest man of his age, if ever that solitary superlative existed, could escape these unfavourable reflections of himself in various small mirrors; and even Milton, looking for his portrait in a spoon, must submit to have the facial angle of a bumpkin.[26]

The mirror here is both spoon-small and as large as society as such: we see ourselves mirrored in the opinions of others, and one of the things Eliot offers here is a psychologically plausible reason for Casaubon's withdrawal from the larger world. Then again, the comparison with Milton—a man intimately engaged in the great events of his time, after all—undercuts Casaubon's rather ridiculous *amour propre*. It is very delicately done by Eliot, I think.

The claim that mimetic art is a mirror of life veers, by its generality, towards platitude. Eliot is always interested in the particular, and her mirrors—her tall standing mirrors in wealthy Middlemarchers' houses, her tuppeny hand-mirrors, her spoons and drops of ink—are all specifying and individuating, even in their distortions and creative rescopings. It is in such terms, I think, that we had better think of the kinds of mirrors, or lenses, that Eliot's epigraphs are.

---

26   Ibid., ch. 10.

One last point, here about epigraphy and the use of quotation and allusion more broadly, concerns originality. *How to be original* is a challenge modern writers face in a way older writers did not. Walter Jackson Bate's venerable study remains a valuable account of the large shift in aesthetic philosophy, from a pre-Romantic belief that the artist was to be judged by its *fidelity* to a set of canonical prototypes, to a Romantic and post-Romantic valorisation of 'originality'. From, that is, an understanding of art as essentially emulative and determined by tradition to one that prizes progress and novelty. By the end of the eighteenth-century, according to Bate:

> The whole concept of 'originality' had both deepened and spread—deepened as a hold on the conscience and spread horizontally among the literate, and the peripheries of the literate, as something desired per se. Back in the 1730s and 1740s, when the neoclassic had begin to reconsider its own self-limitations, the idea of 'originality' had understandably been plucked out into prominence [...] it meshed with some many other things in life aside from the arts (especially the concept of progress in the cumulative sciences, social and historical as well as physical) that the conscience was trapped by it, as it had earlier been trapped by the neoclassic use of the classical example.[27]

Bate notes that '"originality" in the arts need not imply vigour, range, or even openness of mind—or power of language or anything else of a qualitative nature.' What it does, he thinks, is 'lift the burden of the past', or at least attempt to do so.

Do we think of *Middlemarch* as an 'original' novel? Let's say: yes in terms of its scope and achievement, for there had been nothing like it in English before. Then again, perhaps we run the risk of undermining the work's own textual commitment to fidelity by putting too much emphasis on originality, for the counter-argument would be: *Middlemarch* takes its places gladly in a tradition of novel-writing, aiming not at newness for the sake of newness but on the contrary excavating the past, working older modes of wisdom—it is, according to its own logic, a history. And certainly *Middlemarch* is not 'original' in the way that (say) James Joyce's *Ulysses* is—although *Ulysses* is also, in its way, profoundly imbricated in the logic of realism. Nonetheless, it is hard to think of a novel more

---

27   *The Burden of the Past and the English Poet* (London: Chatto and Windus, 1971), pp. 104–05.

concerned with 'the burden of the past' than *Middlemarch*, conceived in political, religious and scientific terms, and actualised emotionally in the plot via Casaubon's mortal attempt to control Dorothea from beyond the grave.

The fabric of Eliot's novel is pinned to its board by a large number of meaningful quotations and epigraphs. We could read these as gestures towards regrounding Eliot's stories in the past from which those micro-texts are sourced; as, that is to say, a strategy at odds with the modern will-to-originality. The claim that Eliot has here written a traditional novel does not, on its face, do any violence to common sense. Nonetheless, the alternative is more compelling, even including the counter-intuitive claim that these epigraphs and quotations are themselves markers *of originality*, rather than the reverse.

The contrast with *Ulysses* might look forced, but it is worth remembering that not everybody greeted the publication of Joyce's novel gladly. D. H. Lawrence famously, or notoriously, dismissed the novel in a letter to Aldous Huxley in pungent terms:

> My God, what a clumsy *olla putrida* James Joyce is! Nothing but old fags and cabbage stumps of quotations from the Bible and the rest, stewed in the juice of deliberate, journalistic dirty-mindedness—what old and hard-worked staleness, masquerading as the all-new![28]

What's interesting here is that Lawrence uses the fact that *Ulysses* is an intensely allusive, quoteful text—which it certainly is—to rebut the notion that it is 'all-new' and original. The one, it seems, negates the other. Never mind the formal, stylistic and mythographic innovation of the novel, Lawrence is saying: how can a work so comprised of fag-end, cabbage-stump quotations pretend to *newness*? The rhetoric shows Lawrence's thumb in the balance, of course: not quotations as such—which might be fragrant yet-to-be-smoked cigarettes, or fresh cabbage leaves ready for cooking—but the leftovers of quotations, the unusable portions here added to the book's metaphorical 'recipe' from sheer perversity, or dirty-mindedness. Even if this were true of Joyce (and I don't think it is) it would not apply to Eliot, whose 'traditional' formal and stylistic textual strategies are enhanced by her epigraphy—much of

---

28   Quoted in Anthony Beal, ed., *D. H. Lawrence: Selected Literary Criticism* (New York: Viking Press, 1956), p. 148

which is original writing by Eliot herself—in a way that discloses, rather than encloses, meaning.

Colin Burrow argues that 'what has tended to be marginalised in the more recent history of imitation is the aspect of it that was most central to the rhetorical tradition', namely 'that is the view that the imitator learns from an *exemplum*: a practice rather than a series of texts or a sequence of words, and that the end of imitation is the acquisition of a habituated skill, rather than a specific set of actions or phrases'. He is less interested in *imitatio*, the strict or even slavish copying of some old master, and more in what he calls *hexis*, the kind of spontaneous skill that comes after long practice and imitation: the way years of scales and laboriously worked-through practice of Beethoven and Chopin finds fruition with the pianist who can so fluently, and seemingly effortlessly, move her hands over the piano keyboard; the expert judgement of the experienced surgeon's cut, or the perfect in-the-moment contact between striker's foot and football to score a goal.[29] Burrow does not discuss *Middlemarch*, though the terminology seems peculiarly fitting to Eliot's mature fiction. On the one hand, Eliot draws, in a distinctly post-Romantic manner, on what we might call 'nature'. Walter Jackson Bate imagines Romantic artists, compelled by a nagging sense that imitation was mere plagiary, despairing of ever being able to free their texts from intertextuality: 'nature—life in all its diversity—is still constantly before us. Cannot we *force* ourselves to turn directly towards it?'[30] There's no question but that Eliot, in writing her novel, drew on her own experience of life in the Midlands, and the people she had encountered. But of course she also drew deeply on literature and literary convention. In part this was a matter of reading novelists themselves informed by the complex Romantic shift from a broader aesthetic of *imitation* to originality: Goethe, Scott, Austen, Dickens, De Staël, George Sand and the like. But she tends to draw her epigraphs, and to make specific intertextual

---

29   Burrow adopts the term from Aristotle, who describes *hexis* as 'an entrenched psychic condition or state which develops through experience rather than congenitally', glossing: 'the successful imitator does not simply learn rules or vocabulary from his master, but acquires through imitation the ability to speak with an instinctive appropriateness'. *Imitating Authors: Plato to Futurity* (Oxford: Oxford University Press, 2019), pp. 5–6, https://doi.org/10.1093/oso/9780198838081.001.0001

30   Bate, *Burden of the Past*, p. 111. His own answer to this rhetorical question is, of course: no—though in the case of Wordsworth, his main focus, a compelling and revolutionary kind of poetic no.

reference, less to these figures than to an older pre-Romantic tradition, older English poetry, Elizabethan-Jacobean drama, Classical literature. In this she is not being derivative so much as she is crediting the larger school at which she honed her *hexis*. Later in his study Burrow defines hexis as a 'habit of healthy fluency' and 'a stably possessed power and disposition to do.'[31] This neatly encapsulates the end-product of Eliot's immersion in literary antecedence. She works her originality (and for the avoidance of doubt, let me say I believe *Middlemarch* is a profoundly original novel) *through* her intertextual inhabitation of *imitatio* of the classics. The latter informs the former.

What we call 'originality' in literature, we call in politics 'revolution', or at the very least 'reform'; and in science we call 'progress', an advance in efficacy or accuracy upon what has gone before. In these senses *Middlemarch* not only works originally, it leverages its originality through its metatextual concurrences. It is a cleverly self-referential meditation upon the very notion of originality itself: originality in religion, in science, in politics and, ultimately, in love.

Adam Phillips quotes Jean Cocteau: 'true originality consists in trying to behave like everybody else without succeeding'. His point, a pertinent one for a novel like *Middlemarch* (although that's not what Phillips is discussing), is that originality is actually a function of a kind of community, or more specifically as a kind of falling away from community: 'it was once,' he argues, 'characteristically modern to idealise originality, and to conceive of it as a form of failure. The fittest as those who didn't fit'. He continues:

> The Romantic concept of genius, after all—the apotheosis of originality—
> was itself a kind of elegy for a lost community. All the solitary, disillusioned
> moderns—Baudelaire, Kafka, Eliot, Beckett—are preoccupied by their
> sociability: its impossibility, its triviality, its compromises, its shame. For
> these writers ambition without irony flies in the face of the evidence;
> a successful life was a contradiction in terms, because the Modernist
> revelation was that lives don't work. A certain revulsion was integral to
> their vision.[32]

Revulsion overstates Eliot's approach, of course; but she certainly shares this insight that the opposite of originality is not 'tradition' so much as

---

31   Burrow, *Imitating Authors*, p. 92.
32   Adam Phillips, 'Getting Ready to Exist', *London Review of Books*, 19.4 (1997), https://
     lrb.co.uk/the-paper/v19/n14/adam-phillips/getting-ready-to-exist

social conformism. As a novel *Middlemarch* construes what another writer might portray as stifling and procrustean about the restrictive dynamics of polite Middlemarchian society in warmer, often comic ways. But that's not to say there's any mistaking them for the claustrophobia-inducing limitations that they are.

The most acute 'originality' in this novel, then, is not Lydgate's failures as a medical researcher, nor Casaubon's failures to revolutionise the study of comparative mythology, both of which lead both men further *into* the thickets of social conformity and convention. It is rather the way Dorothea and Ladislaw are able, at the end, to slip out of the net of the novel's textual society, and therefore out of textuality itself, altogether. It is an original way to end a novel in the bald sense—in the sense that no other writer had thought to in-effect erase their protagonist as the denouement of their story—but more than that, in a deeper sense, it achieves originality through a kind of fidelity, or at least through the assertion of such: for all we are told about Dorothea is that she lives *faithfully* a hidden life, and rests in unvisited tombs. The fidelity is itself pointed up by a literary allusion, to Herodotus, that is as much mythic as it is historical, an allusion discussed below. The larger point is that such quotation and epigraphy are not merely recidivist. On the contrary, they construe a path into a kind of newness, as I argue in what follows.

1. Eliot's Double Mirror

Many of the chapter epigraphs in Middlemarch are quoted from specifically attributed sources: 'Shakespeare', 'Old Song' and so on. Others come without attribution, and in these cases Eliot herself is the author—a snatch of poetry, or an excerpt from an Elizabethan-sounding play, which she is passing-off as a 'quotation'.[1] Take, for instance, the epigraph to Part 8 Chapter 72, near the end of the novel:

> Full souls are double mirrors, making still
> An endless vista of fair things before,
> Repeating things behind.

These words are Eliot's own work. The image of the 'double mirror', though, is not original to her. It comes from Blaise Pascal, via George Sand.

This is interesting for several Eliot-related reasons. Take Sand, for example: George Henry Lewes championed the French novelist, met her in person and encouraged Eliot to read her (in 1842, Lewes wrote that Sand was 'the most remarkable writer of the present century [...] infinitely more than novelist, she is a Poet, not of the head alone, but of the heart'), advice Eliot certainly followed.[2] Indeed, it became something of a commonplace in contemporary critical reactions to Eliot to equate her with Sand.

When Sidney Colvin, in his discerning review of *Daniel Deronda*, remarked, 'the art of fiction has reached its highest point in the hands of

---

1   Surveying Eliot's complete works, David Higdon tabulates all the epigraphs ('or mottoes as George Eliot chose to call them') and arrives at the following numbers: 'There are 225 of them in her works—96 of them original and 129 drawn from the works of fifty-six identified and eight anonymous authors'. 'George Eliot and the Art of the Epigraph', p. 128.

2   Lewes' assessment is quoted in Valerie Dodd, *George Eliot: an Intellectual Life* (Macmillan 1990), p.213

    https://doi.org/10.11647/OBP.0249.01

two women in our time' he was merely echoing a sentiment which had
been expressed many times in the preceding fifteen years.[3]

But while there have been journal articles and even whole PhDs, written
on Eliot and Sand, there has been, to my knowledge, very little on Eliot
and Pascal.[4] This is strange, since we know that Eliot read Pascal's
Pensées avidly from a young age. Pascal provides the epigraph to both
Middlemarch's 33rd and 75th chapters: 'Qui veut délasser hors de propos,
lasse' and 'Le sentiment de la fausseté des plaisirs présents, et l'ignorance
de la vanité des plaisirs absents causent l'inconstance', respectively.
One of the first things we learn about Dorothea, at the beginning of the
very first chapter, is that she 'knew many passages of Pascal's *Pensées*'
by heart, passages which illuminated for her 'the destinies of mankind
[...] by the light of Christianity'. And one of the reasons she considers
marrying Casaubon is that she is able to persuade herself 'it would be
like marrying Pascal. I should learn to see the truth by the same light as
great men have seen it by'.[5] So what of that epigraph to Chapter 72, with
its comparison of 'full souls' to 'double mirrors, making still/an endless
vista of fair things before,/Repeating things behind'?

We know that Eliot read Sand's *Lettres d'un voyageur* (1837). Here's a
relevant passage from the English version of that novel:

> I do not exactly know what Pascal meant by those '*pensées de derrière la
> tête*,' which he reserved as a reply to polemical objections, or for denying
> in secret what he feigned to accept openly. This was most probably, the
> Jesuitism of intellect, forced to bend to outward duty, but nevertheless
> involuntarily rebelling against the absurd decision. To me, the expression
> seemed a terrible one. It has not only been met with amongst his '*Pensées*,'
> but written separately on a piece of paper, and conceived somewhat in
> this way: 'And I also, I shall have my "thoughts from the back of the
> head."' Oh! mournful words, drawn from a desolate heart! Alas! there
> are days when the human heart is like a double mirror, where one

---

3   Patricia Thomson, 'The Three Georges', *Nineteenth-Century Fiction*, 18.2 (1963),
     137–50 (p. 137), https://doi.org/10.1525/ncl.1963.18.2.99p0183d

4   See for example Alexandra K. Wettlaufer, 'George Sand, George Eliot, and the
     Politics of Difference', *The Romanic Review*, 107.1–4 (2016), 77–102, https://doi.
     org/10.1215/26885220-107.1-4.77; Daniel Vitaglione, *George Eliot and George Sand:
     A Comparative Study* (unpublished PhD thesis, University of St Andrews, 1990),
     http://hdl.handle.net/10023/15069

5   Eliot, *Middlemarch*, ch. 3.

surface sends back to the other the reverse of those objects it has received in front.[6]

Sand's image of the human heart as a 'double-mirror' (the original is: 'le cerveau humain est comme un double miroir dont une glace renvoie à l'autre le revers des objets qu'elle a reçus de face') implies facing mirrors each reflecting the other in a kind of *mise-en-abîme*—Eliot's 'endless vista' brings this out. It's clear that Sand's image riffs, explicitly, on Pascal's idea of 'thoughts from the back of the head',[7] and that's an idea that has a manifest resonance for what *Middlemarch* is doing as a novel.

What is at the back of Dorothea's head, so late in the novel as chapter 72? Life has finally freed her from Casaubon, and she is independent and wealthy. 'A husband would not let you have your plans', Celia rebukes her, to which Dorothea snaps: 'As if I wanted a husband!' What plans? To aid Lydgate, caught-up in the scandal of Bulstrode's fall, and widely thought guilty-by-association or perhaps even a co-conspirator, although believed by Dorothea blameless (as, actually, he is). Her brother-in-law and uncle, over dinner, rebuke Dorothea's naivety, but presumably that's not what is referred to by the 'foil or shadow acting like an iron spring within the brain' here. Presumably there's something else going on. The forward part of her head is sure she wants no husband, but the back of her head knows better, and between these two mirrors her soul is cast into its amoureuse, or malamoureuse, *mise-en-abîme*. Dorothea wants her independence, and that independence means the power to choose the partner her heart desires, but choosing Ladislaw means sacrificing her financial security and therefore her independence just as it means acquiring, for a second time, a husband. *As if I wanted a husband!*

Pascal's 72nd *pensée*, 'On Man's Disproportion', includes his celebrated thoughts on the 'double infinity' that frames the human condition, caught as we are between the infinitely large and the infinitely small. Of these 'deux infinis' Pascal insists:

> If we are well informed, we understand that, as nature has graven her image and that of her Author on all things, they almost all partake of her double infinity [...] We naturally believe ourselves far more capable

6   George Sand, *Letters of a Traveller*, trans. by Eliza A. Ashurst (London: Churton, 1847), p. 142

7   Blaise Pascal, *Pensées, introduction by T. S. Eliot* (New York: E. P. Dutton & Co., 1958), https://www.gutenberg.org/files/18269/18269-h/18269-h.htm

of reaching the centre of things than of embracing their circumference. The visible extent of the world visibly exceeds us; but as we exceed little things, we think ourselves more capable of knowing them. And yet we need no less capacity for attaining the Nothing than the All. Infinite capacity is required for both, and it seems to me that whoever shall have understood the ultimate principles of being might also attain to the knowledge of the Infinite. The one depends on the other, and one leads to the other. These extremes meet and reunite by force of distance and find each other in God, and in God alone.

The 'middle' of *Middlemarch* is, as we first take it, a place, a geographical locator: a town in the Midlands, the central territory of this British island. Then, as we read, we understand that the middle of this novel is its subject: neither the aristocracy nor the very poor, neither the extraordinarily virtuous nor the melodramatically wicked. The novel as an aesthetic project calibrated carefully to walk a middling path between fantasy and documentary. But there is, I think, another sense in which the novel middles its vision. In tacit answer to Pascal's question 'Qu'est-ce qu'un homme dans l'infini?' Eliot says: infinite greatness and infinite divisibility both would annihilate us, and so it must be that we are where we are, in the *middle* between these two things. *Middlemarch* is neither concerned with infinitesimals and trivia, nor does it have pretensions to talk in windily cosmic terms. It is a novel about ordinary people and the ordinary things that happen to them, and in this is, precisely, its knowledge of the infinite. It has to be, as the narrator notes in one of the novel's most famous passages, since either of Pascal's infinities could collapse our minds: 'if we had a keen vision and feeling of all ordinary human life, it would be like hearing the grass grow and the squirrel's heart beat and we should die of that roar which lies on the other side of silence. As it is, the quickest of us walk about well wadded with stupidity'.[8]

Pascal finds in our middle-ness a sign of divine providence: 'Car enfin qu'est-ce que l'homme dans la nature?' he asks. What then is man in nature? And he answers himself: 'un néant à l'égard de l'infini, un tout à l'égard du néant, un milieu entre rien et tout'; he is nothing in relation to infinity, and he is everything in relation to nothingness, he is the midpoint between nothing and everything. We are where we

---

8   Eliot, *Middlemarch*, ch. 22.

are, says Pascal, because that is where God has put us: 'la nature ayant gravé son image et celle de son auteur dans toutes choses, elles tiennent presque toutes de sa double infinité'.[9] Nature has engraved its image and that of its Creator in all things; almost everything derives from its double infinity.

Moreover, in arguing that humanity is strung between 'two infinities' Pascal also means that we exist between the infinite stretch of time before our birth and the time that stretches out, infinitely far, after our death. 'When', he says in the *Pensées*

> I consider the short duration of my life, swallowed up in the eternity before and after, the small space which I fill, or even can see, engulfed in the infinite immensity of spaces whereof I know nothing, and which know nothing of me, I am terrified, and wonder that I am here rather than there, for there is no reason why here rather than there, or now rather than then. Who has set me here? By whose order and design have this place and time been destined for me?—*Memoria hospitis unius diei prætereuntis*. It is not well to be too much at liberty. It is not well to have all we want.[10]

'The eternal silence of these infinite spaces alarms me,' shudders Pascal. *Le silence éternel de ces espaces infinis m'effraie*. Eliot, however, is *not* afraid. And that, I think, says something important about her art. As a writer she's really not very interested, as a Joseph Conrad or an Emil Cioran might be, in existential dread and terror. On the contrary: Eliot's 'middle' inverts the Pascalian framing—not, as it might be, a little life surrounded on either side by terrifying infinities of lifelessness, but a little *death*, Casaubon's, bookended by two zones of life, love and hope. Perhaps it looks odd to describe Dorothea's starting point, back in the novel's early chapters as being one of love. I suppose it's more conventional to think of her as just misguided (although it's pretty condescending to Dorothea as a person to tell her, 'no my dear you're not *really* in love with Casaubon, you're just casting around for some way to express your nascent spiritual yearning'). But what if—she isn't? Is it so impossible to believe she actually did love Casaubon? Perhaps, for all her austerity of manner, what most defines Dorothea is precisely a kind of spontaneous excess of love.

---

9   Pascal, *Pensées*, 72.
10 *Pensées*, 205. The Latin is from the apocryphal *Wisdom of Solomon* [5:14]: the King James Version translates this line as '*the remembrance of a guest that tarrieth but a day*'.

With this Pascal-via-George-Sand verse epigraph to the *first* chapter of
Book 8, it is instructive to look at the epigraph to Book 8's (and the
novel's) very *last* chapter. From the soul as a double-mirror we shift to
the heart as preserved in a miraculous supersaturation of love:

> Le cœur se sature d'amour comme d'un sel divin qui le conserve; de là
> l'incorruptible adhérence de ceux qui se sont aimés des l'aube de la vie,
> et la fraicheur des vielles amours prolongés. Il existe un embaumement
> d'amour. C'est de Daphnis et Chlöe que sont faits Philémon et Baucis.
> Cette vieillesse là, ressemblance du soir avec l'aurore.—VICTOR HUGO:
> *L'homme qui rit.*

> The heart is saturated with love as with a divine salt that preserves it;
> there is an incorruptible coherence to those who have loved in the dawn
> of their life that brings freshness to old, long-lasting loves. It is, as it were,
> an embalming of love. It is out of Daphnis and Chloe that Philemon
> and Baucis are made. In such an old age, the evening harks back to the
> dawn.—VICTOR HUGO: *The Man Who Laughs.*

This is Eliot's inversion—her mirror image, we could say—of Pascal's
two, terrifying eternities of blankness: a life bookended by love and
preserved by the connection, the reflection, of the one in the other.
It's a heartening way of looking at life, and long-term relationships;
but it is also the way Eliot has chosen to frame her novel. The shape of
Middlemarch is a death between two loves.

The novel's 'Finale', Eliot's epilogue, presents itself to the reader
without any epigraph. But it still, by way of concluding Dorothea's
story, or more precisely by way of declining exactly to conclude her
story, manages to strike a beautiful, plangent note. Ends, says Eliot,
are beginnings, and neither is the terrifying eternity of silence that so
affrighted Pascal. 'Every limit is a beginning as well as an ending [...]
marriage, which has been the bourne of so many narratives, is still a
great beginning'. Dorothea cannot live as a grand heroic Theresa or
Antigone, Eliot tells us, because 'the medium in which their ardent
deeds took shape is forever gone'—but a new, quotidian medium has
come about, just as dramatically and morally engaging. 'Medium' in the
sense of environment becomes medium in the sense of middle.

> Her finely touched spirit had still its fine issues, though they were not
> widely visible. Her full nature, like that river of which Cyrus broke the
> strength, spent itself in channels which had no great name on the earth.

But the effect of her being on those around her was incalculably diffusive: for the growing good of the world is partly dependent on unhistoric acts; and that things are not so ill with you and me as they might have been, is half owing to the number who lived faithfully a hidden life, and rest in unvisited tombs.[11]

So I revert to my earlier question—in the middle of what?—by picking up the suggestion that one of the things this great novel mediates is a kind of mutual doubled speculum. I have already touched upon the commonplace by which 'the mirror' has long been a trope of art as such, and 'realism', that complicated term, such as Eliot writes is supposed precisely to hold, as it were, the mirror up to nature. Eliot's self-reflexive textual mirrors, though, tend to be more complex than a simple foursquare reflection. And I have already quoted *Adam Bede*'s Escher-like opening image:

With a single drop of ink for a mirror, the Egyptian sorcerer undertakes to reveal to any chance comer far-reaching visions of the past. This is what I undertake to do for you, reader. With this drop of ink at the end of my pen, I will show you the roomy workshop of Mr. Jonathan Burge, carpenter and builder, in the village of Hayslope, as it appeared on the eighteenth of June, in the year of our Lord 1799.[12]

But the *Middlemarch*-ian mirror, via its Pascalian doubling, involves a still more complex narrative strategy, because it is deliberately self-reflexive. Eliot's novel is both a reflection, scrupulously researched, of an English Midlands town in the late 1820s and 1830s, and a self-reflection, a meditation on the scope and nature of Eliot's own art—as in the novel's famous last paragraphs. The impossible Pascalian 'infinity' that frames the project of realism (what George Henry Lewes pegged as 'Truthism', and which he opposed 'not to Idealism but to *Falsism*')[13] is, surely, the idea of total vision.

The perfect mirror would reflect everything, just as the perfect realist novel would capture everything. Impossibilities, both, of course. Eliot's double mirror, though, by turning on itself shrinks that bad infinity down into itself. Eliot achieves her total vision by not attempting totality,

---

11   Eliot, *Middlemarch*, 'Finale'.
12   Eliot, *Adam Bede*, ch. 1.
13   George Henry Lewes, 'Realism in Art: Recent German Fiction', *Westminster Review*, 70 (1858), 493–94.

as when she so elegantly and deliberately steps away as narrator from the latter phase of Dorothea's life. Fredric Jameson wonders whether 'the bad totalization projected by Casaubon's *Key to All Mythologies*' isn't 'the caricature and distorted mirror image of Eliot's own achieved totalization in *Middlemarch* itself'.[14] It's an argument with some appeal, except that a key is a different kind of thing to a mirror.

It has to do, I think, with Eliot's deftness, the way her writing both convincingly 'reflects' the world she is describing (in the sense that she compels readerly belief in that world) and 'self-reflects' on her own practice as she goes along. Her praxis becomes part of her world, and the world becomes part of her praxis. It is a complex mimesis, I think, and richer and more compelling than the plainer Zola-esque or Gissing-y realism discussed above.

How is a key different to a mirror? Critics have explored the extent to which Eliot based her Casaubon upon her contemporary Mark Pattison, the brilliant intellect and Rector of Lincoln College Oxford whose sexless, miserable marriage and ultimate failure to capitalise upon his youthful scholarly potential find parallels in Eliot's character. Among the harder to ignore parallels between Pattison and Casaubon is that Pattison actually published a book *on* Casaubon—Isaac Casaubon, that is, the sixteenth-century Swiss theologian.[15] Pattison's Casaubon,

---

14 Fredric Jameson, *The Antimonies of Realism* (London: Verso Books, 2014), pp. 133–34

15 See for instance, H. S. Jones, *Intellect and Character in Victorian England: Mark Pattison and the Invention of the Don* (Cambridge: Cambridge University Press, 2007), https://doi.org/10.1017/cbo9780511660283 and A. D. Nuttall, *Dead from the Waist Down. Scholars and Scholarship in Literature and the Popular Imagination* (New Haven: Yale University Press, 2003). 'Early in 1869 Frances Pattison was introduced to George Eliot. Their friendship blossomed and by late summer they were on intimate terms. In November 1870, five months after a memorable visit to the Pattisons in Oxford, Eliot began work on the story of Dorothea Brooke. Since the publication of *Middlemarch*, readers and critics have speculated about the extent to which Dorothea's arid union with Casaubon was modelled on the failed marriage of Mark and Frances Pattison. The relative ages of the partners, the husband's prematurely withered appearance ("his deep eye-sockets, those two white moles with hairs on them, a bitterness in the mouth and a venom in the glance"), and of course the name Casaubon itself, all suggest a deliberate likeness. In public, Frances Pattison, who remained on good terms with Eliot, always denied having read the book, but Dilke stated plainly, on his wife's authority, that "the religious side of Dorothea Brooke was taken by George Eliot from the letters of Mrs. Pattison," and that Casaubon's letter proposing marriage to Dorothea "at the beginning of the fifth chapter in *Middlemarch*, from what George Eliot herself told me in 1875, must have been very near the letter that Pattison actually wrote, and the reply very much the same"'. Peter Thonemann, 'Wall of Ice', *London Review of Books*, 30.3 (2008), 23–24.

not unlike Eliot's Casaubon, hesitated in the face of the attempt at systematic or complete knowledge, and if the historical Casaubon, at least according to Pattison, did so for reasons of more spiritual cogency than either intellectual timidity or lack of subject knowledge, the final result is not all that different.

> The depreciation of his own performance, which was one of Casaubon's mental habits, was founded on the disparagement of secular knowledge in comparison of piety. But it was further connected with that oppression of mind, which the infinity of knowledge lays upon its votaries. [...] The thought *quantum est quod nescimus* ['how small the amount we can know']—Heinsius' motto—keeps him not only humble, but despondent. Even in science, some of the greatest men have shared the sense of baffled endeavour. Newton's pebbles on the sea-shore are become proverbial. Laplace's dying words were, 'l'homme ne poursuit que de chimères' ['mankind pursues nothing but chimeras'] [...] Research is infinite; it can never be finished.[16]

This glosses the nature of research, but it does more: it construes the character of the researcher, and as such it speaks to another of Eliot's prime concerns in this novel: character. In her account of the novel, Gillian Beer stresses how 'Eliot emphasises the congruity between all the various processes of the imagination, the novelist's and the scientist's', adding that she articulates an 'imagery of transcendence': 'the microscope and the telescope, by making realisable the plurality of worlds, of scales and existences beyond the reach of our particular sense organisation were a powerful antidote to that form of positivism which refused to acknowledge possibilities beyond the present and apparent world'.[17] It is an insight that leads nicely into an examination of the microscopic potency of Eliot's characterisation in this novel. A key opens a door, a linear operation; a lens opens in a more fractal mode, whole new vistas and worlds: the connection not of finitude to finitude, but our mortal limitation to something infinite. A fragment is an incompleteness, but 'it can never be finished' is not the same thing as 'it is mortal', and Eliot's focus is always on this latter and never on the potsherd, the remnant, the eighteenth-century folly. The past, for her, lives in the present, or else it is a kind of inertness.

---

16   Mark Pattison, *Isaac Casaubon 1559–1614* (London: Longmans, Green and Co., 1875), p. 59

17   Gillian Beer, *Darwin's Plots: Evolutionary Narrative in Darwin, George Eliot and Nineteenth-Century Fiction* (London: Routledge and Kegan Paul, 1983), pp. 151–52

2. Sappho's Apple

To step back from the last book of *Middlemarch* to the first. Eliot's story opens with the general expectation among her friends and family that Dorothea will marry Sir James Chettam, the eligible and hearty if rather dim young baronet. This, of course, does not happen. Instead she becomes betrothed to Casaubon. But if Dorothea and Casaubon are mismatched, Dorothea and Sir James would have been just as ill-suited to one another, if in a different way, and surely everybody in the novel knows as much. Still, matchmaker Mrs. Cadwallader is not thereby discouraged:

> It followed that Mrs. Cadwallader must decide on another match for Sir James, and having made up her mind that it was to be the younger Miss Brooke, there could not have been a more skilful move towards the success of her plan than her hint to the baronet that he had made an impression on Celia's heart. For he was not one of those gentlemen who languish after the unattainable Sappho's apple that laughs from the topmost bough.[1]

We take the point of her allusion: Sir James is a down-to-earth fellow, not the sort to go mooning after unattainable women.

Where did Eliot come across the 'Sappho's apple' reference? It is from Karl Otfried Müller's *History of the Literature of Ancient Greece to the Period of Isocrates*, which had appeared in English in 1840—translated by the man who was, a few years after its publication, to become Eliot's lover, and whom she considered her husband, George Henry Lewes. This is what Lewes's Müller says:

> In a fragment lately discovered, which bears a strong impression of the simple language of Sappho, she compares the freshness of youth and the

---

1   Eliot, *Middlemarch*, ch. 6.

    https://doi.org/10.11647/OBP.0249.02

unsullied beauty of a maiden's face to an apple of some peculiar kind, which, when all the rest of the fruit is gathered from the tree, remains alone at an unattainable height, and drinks in the whole vigour of vegetation; or rather (to give the simple words of the poetess in which the thought is placed before us and gradually heightened with great beauty and nature): 'like the sweetapple which ripens at the top of the bough, on the topmost point of the bough, forgotten by the gatherers—no, not quite forgotten, but beyond their reach'.[2]

Müller adds a footnote: 'the fragment is in Walz, *Rhetores Graeci*, vol. viii. p. 883' and quotes the Greek:

οἶον τὸ γλυκύμαλον ἐρυεθεται ἄκρῳ ἐπ ὔσδῳ,
ἄκρον ἐπ ἀκροτάτῳ, λελάθοντο δὲ μαλοδρόπηες,
οὐ μὰν ἐκλελάθοντ᾽ἀλλ᾽ οὐκ ἐδύναντ ἐπίκεσθαι …

Sappho may have written as many as 10,000 lines of poetry, although today fewer than seven hundred lines survive. Despite her once widespread popularity, she fell out of favour in the centuries after her death, either because the Aeolic dialect of Greek in which she wrote came to be considered ugly, or else because of disapproval by the Christian church at her bisexuality. For most of the last thousand years Sappho has been known only by those poems and fragments that happened to be recorded by other writers: one whole poem, three partial poems and various shorter fragments and pieces, down (sometimes) to single words. Sappho's poems had been extracted from these sources and published in separate volumes as early as the 1550s, and in 1681 the French scholar Anne Le Fèvre published an edition of Sappho that made her work more widely known across Europe. Then, in 1879, a papyrus containing a new fragment of Sappho was discovered at Faiyum in Egypt. Many more papyri have been discovered since that date, and our knowledge of Sappho is more extensive nowadays than at any time since classical antiquity. But such 'new' Sappho poems lay in the future as Eliot wrote *Middlemarch*.

Nonetheless, Müller in the 1840s describes Sappho's apple poem as 'a fragment lately discovered'. He does so, despite the fact that he was writing long before the discovery of any new Sappho papyri. How so?

---

2   Karl Otfried Müller, *History of the Literature of Ancient Greece*, trans. by George Cornewall Lewis (London: n.p., 1840), 178–79.

Because another scholar, Christian Walz, had worked through collections of unpublished manuscripts kept in various libraries and private collections in various European cities and in doing so had discovered a number of previously unknown words, lines and passages quoted by the manuscripts' authors. Walz published these in a book called *Rhetores graeci*, 'Rhetoricians of Greece', a work which appeared simultaneously in Stuttgart, London and Paris. Much of what Walz had discovered was fairly dull, but some bits and pieces were more exciting—for instance, the three-line poem Müller quotes, which Walz had found in Syrianus's commentary on Hermogenes' *On Forms* (4th century BCE). Walz does not specifically identify this verse as being by Sappho (hence Müller's caution: 'a fragment which bears a strong impression of the simple language of Sappho') although modern scholars are happier to make the attribution on the grounds of its dialect and closeness to the other things we know Sappho wrote.

When, precisely, was this 'fragment lately discovered' discovered? You can see for yourself with Walz's title page (see Fig. 1)

1832: just the period in which *Middlemarch* is set. This reference to 'Sappho's apple', which Eliot came across in the book her lover had translated into English, could hardly be, in terms of the imagined world of *Middlemarch*, more up-to-date. A brand-new portion of Sappho had come into the world just as Eliot's story is unfolding, and her narrator knows all about it.

It is, in other words, another instance of the scrupulousness and precision with which Eliot undertook the research that undergirds her novel. This aspect of her creative praxis has become, for good reason, one of the axioms of Eliot scholarship.[3] And if part of that labour was in the service of what we might call, though it is a slippery term, 'verisimilitude'—creating the textual conditions into which readers might safely suspend their disbelief in a positive sense, with precisely observed detail, and in a negative by avoiding the kinds of errors that 'bounce' a reader out of her faith in the story—another part consisted in assembling a matrix of textual reference, like this Sappho allusion, in which the story of *Middlemarch* itself might be situated and fortified.

---

3   See for instance, Meg M. Moring, 'George Eliot's Scrupulous Research: The Facts behind Eliot's Use of the "Keepsake in *Middlemarch*"', *Victorian Periodicals Review*, 26.1 (1993), 19–23 and Jerome Beaty, *Middlemarch from Notebook to Novel: A Study of George Eliot's Creative Method* (Illinois: University of Illinois Press, 1960).

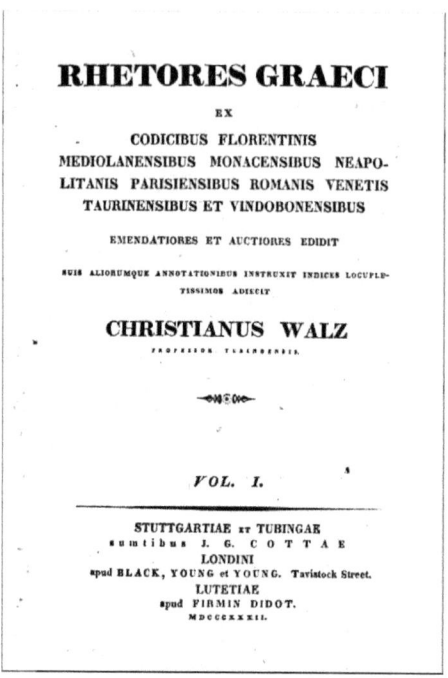

Fig. 1 Christianus Walz, *Rhetores Graeci*, vol. 1 (Stuttgart and Tubingen: J. G. Cotta, 1832), title page, https://www.google.co.uk/books/edition/Rhetores_Graeci_ex_codicibus_Florentinis/KzTGebC5F6gC?hl=en&gbpv=1. Public domain.

The apple, here, is Dorothea Brooke (it is perhaps not coincidental that the 'west brook' is a variety of hard, speckled apple popular in the nineteenth-century), but also it is Eliot's particular correlative for human love, not as a heavenly ideal, and neither down in the dirt, or too easily apprehended. Later in the novel, in another of the story's three love stories, Fred Vincy rides to the house of Mary Garth, whom he loves. The occasion for the visit is that, having misjudged the sale of a horse, he is out of pocket. He owes a debt of £160 which Mary's father has co-signed, and he can only pay back £50, even though the shortfall might ruin Mr. Garth. 'But for Mary's existence and Fred's love for her', Eliot tells us, 'his conscience would have been much less active both in previously urging the debt on his thought and impelling him not to spare himself after his usual fashion by deferring an unpleasant task, but to act as directly and simply as he could'. So he rides out:

> The Garth family, which was rather a large one, for Mary had four brothers and one sister, were very fond of their old house, from which all the best furniture had long been sold. Fred liked it too, knowing it by heart even to the attic which smelt deliciously of apples and quinces, and until to-day he had never come to it without pleasant expectations.[4]

Apples (plus quinces) are again elevated as a sign of the not-immediately-accessible love object, here located in the bourgeois comfort of a spacious house (such material considerations also being part of Mary's appeal to Fred). First, though, he must 'make his confession before Mrs. Garth, of whom he was rather more in awe than of her husband'—and whom, significantly, he encounters in the kitchen 'her sleeves turned above her elbows [...] pinching an apple-puff'—although she is herself described in terms of a different fruit, or fruit product: 'the passage from governess into housewife had wrought itself a little too strongly into her consciousness [...] the exemplary Mrs. Garth had her droll aspects, but her character sustained her oddities, as a very fine wine sustains a flavour of skin'. Apples more than once symbolically situate the Edenic possibilities offered, for Fred and also for Farebrother, represented by marriage to Mary and a place in amongst the Garths:

> Caleb, rather tired with his day's work, was seated in silence with his pocket-book open on his knee, while Mrs. Garth and Mary were at their sewing, and Letty in a corner was whispering a dialogue with her doll, Mr. Farebrother came up the orchard walk, dividing the bright August lights and shadows with the tufted grass and the apple-tree boughs.[5]

Farebrother, when he recognises that Mary loves not him but Fred, eventually does the decent thing. Still, one of the things Eliot is doing here is contrasting the elevated Sapphic of Dorothea with the more figuratively and literally down-to-earth apple of Mary Garth.

> Mr. Farebrother left the house soon after, and seeing Mary in the orchard with Letty, went to say good-by to her. They made a pretty picture in the western light which brought out the brightness of the apples on the old scant-leaved boughs—Mary in her lavender gingham and black ribbons holding a basket, while Letty in her well-worn nankin picked up the fallen apples. If you want to know more particularly how Mary looked, ten to one you will see a face like hers in the crowded street

---

4   Eliot, *Middlemarch*, ch. 24.
5   Ibid., ch. 40.

to-morrow [...] some small plump brownish person of firm but quiet carriage, who looks about her, but does not suppose that anybody is looking at her. If she has a broad face and square brow, well-marked eyebrows and curly dark hair, a certain expression of amusement in her glance which her mouth keeps the secret of, and for the rest features entirely insignificant—take that ordinary but not disagreeable person for a portrait of Mary Garth. [...] Mary admired the keen-faced handsome little Vicar in his well-brushed threadbare clothes more than any man she had had the opportunity of knowing [...] it was remarkable that the actual imperfections of the Vicar's clerical character never seemed to call forth the same scorn and dislike which she showed beforehand for the predicted imperfections of the clerical character sustained by Fred Vincy. Will any one guess towards which of those widely different men Mary had the peculiar woman's tenderness?—the one she was most inclined to be severe on, or the contrary? 'Have you any message for your old playfellow, Miss Garth?' said the Vicar, as he took a fragrant apple from the basket which she held towards him, and put it in his pocket. 'Something to soften down that harsh judgment? I am going straight to see him.'[6]

Farebrother takes the apple, but Fred, Mary's old playfellow, gets the girl. And when Fred calls, later in the novel, to plight his troth, it will not surprise us that he encounters the Garths, 'the family group, dogs and cats included, under the great apple-tree in the orchard'.[7] Eliot provides us with one last twist on this fructal theme. In her epilogue, by way of gratifying her reader's curiosity as to what has happened with her main characters, Eliot confides:

There were three boys: Mary was not discontented that she brought forth men-children only; and when Fred wished to have a girl like her, she said, laughingly, 'that would be too great a trial to your mother.' Mrs. Vincy in her declining years, and in the diminished lustre of her housekeeping, was much comforted by her perception that two at least of Fred's boys were real Vincys, and did not 'feature the Garths.' But Mary secretly rejoiced that the youngest of the three was very much what her father must have been when he wore a round jacket, and showed a marvellous nicety of aim in playing at marbles, or in throwing stones to bring down the mellow pears.[8]

---

6   Ibid.
7   Ibid., ch. 57.
8   Ibid., 'Finale'.

The shift from apples to pears marks the natural development from generation to generation. There is, I suppose, *some* piquancy in the allusion to Lady Macbeth (in the reference to exclusively male children) there; although we can take this as a kind of irony. Few characters in literature are less Lady-Macbeth-like than Mary Garth, after all. At the same time there is something more than adventitious in the juxtaposition of Sappho and Shakespeare in Eliot's textual matrix. The out-of-reach apple of Sappho stands for potential, for the start (perhaps) of something, just as the Edenic apple stands at the mythic start of everything. But Macbeth telling his wife that she should bring forth men-children only[9] looks forward to an eventuality that the play closes-down. It is, in other words, the end of something—an end in which Lady Macbeth leaping to her death from the castle battlements, like Sappho leaping to her death from the cliffs of Lesbos, identifies as having to do with despair, derangement and femaleness. Or to put it a slightly different way, *Macbeth* is a play about the consequences of our actions. That looks, perhaps, like an over-facile summary of Shakespeare's great drama, but it need not. Lady Macbeth, to a much greater extent than her husband, believes her actions will be both beneficial to her and consequence-free. Accordingly it is Lady Macbeth who proves haunted by the fallout of her choices. *Middlemarch* avoids, of course, the grand guignol of *Macbeth* in terms of bodily violence, but it is just as tightly focused on moral violence, and reputational violence, as Shakespeare's play.

There's another layer here, which has to do with the larger enframing assumptions different modes bring to a novel like *Middlemarch*. It is a mode of documentary verisimilitude, and it is an exemplary drama, a myth. Fruit imagery in this novel might be read 'mythically', via Biblical narratives of the fall of man, or Greek-mythological narratives (Atalanta's golden apple, Sappho's high-growing apple, Hesperidean treasure), or 'scientifically', as the mechanism by which trees make more trees, the vehicle of inheritance as such. The cultural—and, as we'll see with other epigraphs and allusions, spiritual—inheritance of *Middlemarch* is located in a web of intertextuality.

---

9   William Shakespeare, *Macbeth*, I. 7. 73.

3. Lydgate Winces

Character and Realism

I would like to talk a little more about middles. Middlemarch is a medium place, and *Middlemarch* a medium novel. 'Medium' means both middle (in a statistical, but also a general sense) and also environment, surround, that inside which we subsist. For biologists a medium is a nutrient solution for the growth of cells in vitro, which growth might of course be observed through a microscope. For plankton, brine is their medium. In a different sense, for human beings, as social creatures, society is our medium. For chemistry and physics 'medium' refers to the surrounding environment (solid, liquid, gas) or to the vacuum through which signals, waves or forces pass.

The second book of *Middlemarch* is about, amongst other things, Lydgate settling himself into his new life. He has grand ambitions for his medical research, looks forward to establishing the new hospital and is generally *restless*.

> But whichever way Lydgate began to incline, there was something to make him wince; and being a proud man, he was a little exasperated at being obliged to wince. He did not like frustrating his own best purposes by getting on bad terms with Bulstrode; he did not like voting against Farebrother [...] he, with his unmixed resolutions of independence and his select purposes, would find himself at the very outset in the grasp of petty alternatives.[1]

Why does he wince? In this specific case, it is because he has a say in whom should be chaplain of the new hospital, and he is torn between voting for his friend, Farebrother (and so alienating the powerful Bulstrode) or voting for Bulstrode's preferred candidate, Tyke, and disappointing

---

1   Eliot, *Middlemarch*, ch. 18.

    https://doi.org/10.11647/OBP.0249.03

his friend. In the end, Lydgate succumbs to the larger social forces and gives up his purely personal preference in favour of Tyke. But as the novel goes on we will see that Lydgate, despite his pride, intelligence and drive, often winces.

One of the reasons Lydgate likes Farebrother is that the two men share a passion for amateur science. In Chapter 17 Farebrother shows Lydgate round his collections of biological specimens, insects and the like. Lydgate takes a liking to an item in the vicar's collection and offers to swap it for something from his own:

> 'I have some sea-mice—fine specimens—in spirits. And I will throw in Robert Brown's new thing—'Microscopic Observations on the Pollen of Plants'—if you don't happen to have it already.'[2]

This is the pamphlet he's talking about.

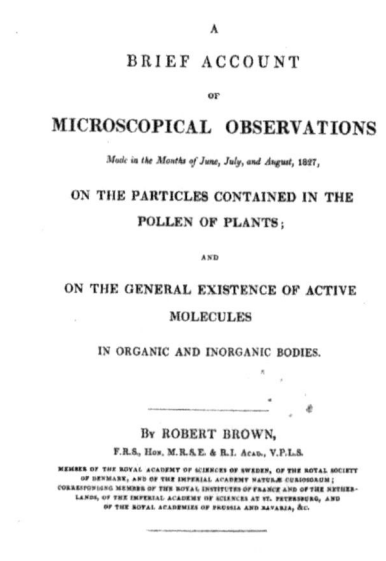

Fig. 2 Robert Brown, *A Brief Account of Microscopical Observations on the Particles Contained in the Pollen of Plants; and On the General Existence of Active Molecules in Organic and Inorganic Bodies* ([n.p.], 1828), title page, https://www.google.co.uk/books/edition/A_Brief_Account_of_Microscopical_Observa/bz8-AAAAcAAJ?hl=en&gbpv=1. Public domain.

---

2   Ibid., ch. 17.

As you can see from the title page, this pamphlet was never published. Brown had it privately printed (in 1828) and distributed copies to his friends. Eliot is once again precisely situating her book in its time. If Lydgate has a copy of Brown's 'new thing' it must be because he is a friend of Brown's, or otherwise in Brown's circle.

It is, nonetheless, an extremely famous work. This pamphlet contains important and influential observations concerning the medium through which we all, speaking physically, move. Even though he did not press them upon the public, Brown's ideas were widely discussed and proved profoundly influential through the century. It concerns what we now call, after its author, 'Brownian motion': the agitation of pollen particles as visible under magnification. Lots of us have done this experiment at school (I certainly did): watch through a microscope as individual pollen grains jiggle and tremble. They move because they are being continually struck on all sides by the much smaller nitrogen, oxygen and carbon-dioxide molecules that constitute the air, and which are themselves in constant motion.

When Brown first observed 'Brownian motion' he could not explain the agitation of the pollen grains he was observing. Indeed, it was not until the beginning of the twentieth century that the real reason was uncovered. All Brown knew is that pollen grains, observed through a powerful microscope, shimmered with movement. The *Edinburgh Journal of Science*, reviewing Brown's pamphlet in 1829, speculated as to the causes of 'the phenomena of motion, which Mr. Brown left enveloped in a sort of mystery, by representing them as inherent in the molecules of organic and inorganic bodies'.[3] Various explanations were proposed, including the theory that the pollen was alive (like spermatozoa), that the motion was electrical in origin, or else that it represented some process of evaporation or other agitation in the medium. The question was energetically debated through the century, although it wasn't until long after Eliot's death that the true cause of Brownian motion was definitively established, by Albert Einstein in 1904.[4]

---

3   M. Raspail, 'Note on Mr Brown's Microscopical Observations on the active Molecules of organic and inorganic bodies', *Edinburgh Journal of Science*, 10 (1829), 106–08 (p. 106).

4   For those interested: the true cause has to do with the kinetic nature of temperature. What we perceive as heat and cold are substrates of atoms moving more or less rapidly. The agitation of pollen grains (tiny to us, but vastly larger than the atoms that make up the air) is them being struck on all sides by these moving and ricocheting atomic particles.

What Brown showed was *that* individual miniscule pollen grains are in constant motion, jiggling from side to side—continually wincing, we might say. He wasn't able to show *why* they were. That was enough for the phenomenon to be named after him. Darwin's achievement later in the century was similar: he argued that evolution happened, but, lacking any knowledge of genetics or the existence of DNA, could not say how hereditable traits were passed down.

Eliot includes this reference to Brown's pamphlet partly because it is chronologically on-point for the 1828–32 timeline of her novel. But I think she is doing something more. It is not just period specific window-dressing: this pamphlet speaks to the way Eliot conceives of character as such. Consider Lydgate. He has grand ambitions, a moral compass and a sense of duty, he is clever and energetic, but he is, for all that, a strangely *passive* individual, knocked back and forth by the miniature forces of this miniature society. The novel does not pretend to explain, in any radical sense, *why* this is the case, but it observes that it *is* the case, for him, and also for almost all the people whose stories it tells.

This is, I think, the best way of approaching the rather garish inset story from Lydgate's past, narrated in chapter 15. In France, we're told, young Lydgate fell in love with a beautiful, married actress, Mme Laure: 'a Provençale, with dark eyes, a Greek profile, and rounded majestic form'. We're told that 'Lydgate was in love with this actress, as a man is in love with a woman whom he never expects to speak to' until one day, on stage in Paris, she stabs her actor-husband to death in front of the audience. This action follows the playscript and Laure is not prosecuted: the legal authorities decide that she slipped and accidentally killed her husband when she was supposed to be only pretending to do so. Since he happens to be present in the audience at this death, Lydgate leaps onto the stage and cradles Mme Laure (she has fallen and hit her head). Afterwards he pays suit to her, eventually proposing marriage. But she refuses him:

> 'I will tell you something,' she said, in her cooing way, keeping her arms folded. 'My foot really slipped.'
>
> 'I know, I know,' said Lydgate, deprecatingly. 'It was a fatal accident—a dreadful stroke of calamity that bound me to you the more.'
>
> Again Laure paused a little and then said, slowly, '*I meant to do it.*'
>
> Lydgate, strong man as he was, turned pale and trembled: moments seemed to pass before he rose and stood at a distance from her.

'There was a secret, then,' he said at last, even vehemently. 'He was brutal to you: you hated him.'

'No! he wearied me; he was too fond: he would live in Paris, and not in my country; that was not agreeable to me.'

'Great God!' said Lydgate, in a groan of horror. 'And you planned to murder him?'

'I did not plan: it came to me in the play—*I meant to do it.*'

Lydgate stood mute, and unconsciously pressed his hat on while he looked at her. He saw this woman—the first to whom he had given his young adoration—amid the throng of stupid criminals.

'You are a good young man,' she said. 'But I do not like husbands. I will never have another.'[5]

This gruesome narrative inset comports oddly, I think, with the carefully proportionate psychological and practical verisimilitude of the rest of *Middlemarch*. It is a little islet of melodrama in an Eliotic sea of more scrupulous literary realism. But it says something interesting about character, and more specifically about the sorts of characters that more usually inhabit Eliot's universe. Mme Laure is a creature driven by a will strong enough to commit murder. She acted not (which Lydgate could have understood and condoned) by accident, nor because she had been driven to murder by an abusive husband—two versions of character passivity—but, on the contrary, *because she wanted to act*, out of a perfect and pitiless agency. She was no pollen grain, jiggled around by mysterious forces, but rather a nexus of volitional action. It is this fact, as much as the crime she has committed, that repels Lydgate I think. And there is a canniness in Eliot's vision here too: looking forward to Lydgate's (at this point) in-the-future falling in love with another woman as implacably wilful and—crucially—as psychologically *opaque* as Laure.

But, Eliot is saying, these are the exceptions in humankind. Most people exist primarily in ways defined by the networks of other people, and are subject, as Lydgate himself is, to the buffeting forces of other people's energies: their desires, their pressures and anxieties and angers, the push-me-pull-you of mutual obligations and gratifications that are, in Eliot's artistic vision, the predominance of human existence. Most of us are small beings in a big world, visible to the novelist's microscope as oscillating grains in the medium.

---

5   Eliot, *Middlemarch*, ch. 15.

At the time she was writing Eliot didn't know for sure (any more than did the world's scientists) what caused Brownian motion. But she knew theories were divided between those that argued the pollen moved because of some motile agency or power or its own, and those that argued the pollen was a passive object *being moved* by forces around it—electrical, atmospheric or something else. It is not that I'm suggesting that she has written Lydgate as a merely passive individual, only acted upon and lacking all independent will or spirit—he would be a very dull character in such a case. But it is, I think, part of Eliot's genius to understand that our will is, by and large, unequal to the various, systemic and complex pressures of our environments. The heroes of epic, romance or melodrama—like Mme Laure—*act* to a greater extent than they are acted upon: they manifest a commanding will, they cut their various Gordian knots and master, or mistress, their destinies. The heroes and heroines of the Realist Novel, though, find life more complicated and restrictive, because actual life, such as we all live it, *is* more complicated and restrictive. The step from the little inset story of Mme Laure to the larger unfolding of Lydgate's story in *Middlemarch* is a shift in *mode*, from one kind of story to another.

And in this latter sense, of what it is Eliot brings to the 'realist' mode of novel-writing, I do think there is something distinctive in her as a realist that has to do with her conception of character. We could compare what another giant of 'Literary Realism' does with character: Leo Tolstoy. We know Tolstoy had a high regard for Eliot's writing: in 1891 he wrote to his publisher, Mikhail Lederle, with a list of forty-five books that impressed him 'most of all', and alongside Homer, the Bible and various others he listed 'novels by the English writer George Eliot'— all of them, perhaps. Early in *Anna Karenina*, Anna is travelling by train and reading 'an English novel'; she imagines herself living the life of the heroine 'caring for a sick man, making speeches in Parliament and riding to hounds'[6]—I've always assumed that she's reading *Middlemarch*, and mixing up in her imagination Dorothea, Ladislaw and Rosamond.

My point here is that Tolstoy is a very different *sort* of realist to Eliot. Here, I am not simply referring to the scope or scale of a novel

---

6   Leo Tolstoy, *Anna Karenina*, trans. by Constance Garnett (New York: Random House, 1939), Part 1, ch. 27, https://www.gutenberg.org/files/1399/1399-h/1399-h.htm

like *War and Peace* when compared to Eliot's more modest panoramas. That obviously is a difference, but a more important one, I think, is that Tolstoy conceives of character as more radically *passive* than did Eliot. Part of the point of *War and Peace* is to show History steamrollering over all its characters, whether or not they think they are ready. Nobody acts in that novel, everybody reacts: the large dramatis personae is spread out on a continuum between, on the one hand, the hapless, likeable and fundamentally passive Pierre and, on the other, Napoleon, the closest the novel comes to a villain. Napoleon thinks he is the embodiment of Hegel's 'World Spirit', but he is not: he is as much swept along by the vastly larger, suprahuman forces of history as anybody else. Indeed, when he's finished telling his story Tolstoy adds a massive appendix detailing his idiosyncratic Theory of History, which is, in a nutshell, that *nobody*, no matter how grand or apparently powerful they are, has any power over History. We are all helpless pollen-grains in Tolstoy's vision of things: buffeted by the forces of love and sex (in *Anna Karenina*), of society, history and war (in *War and Peace*) and of God (in *Resurrection*). One of Tolstoy's most powerful works, 1886's *The Death of Ivan Ilyich*, tells the story of a man who does nothing at all except lie on his bed dying, enduring the passage and finally passing on. Ivan Ilyich may be the most strictly passive fictional character ever written.

It seems to me that, by comparison, Eliot reserves more of a place for will and indeed for wilfulness in her conception of the human character. Not all the people in her fiction simply and passively wait: some act rather than react, and some of those who act do so against the strong current of societal disapproval. At the same time Eliot does not see the world as a melodrama inhabited by Mme Laures, forever on the verge of plunging a knife into their husbands' hearts. Most of us are carried along by life, and deal with things as best we can. One way we can engage with Eliot's fiction is as an exploration of the *mix* between activity and passivity in the human soul. These are, after all, genuinely enduring questions. To what extent are our lives defined by our action, and to what extent by reaction? Are we agents or patients, forceful focal-points of will and agency, or pollen-grains jiggling and trembling from a thousand invisible and often contrary forces? *Middlemarch* gives us the chance to peer through the glass of Eliot's crisply focalising prose at, amongst others, Lydgate. See: he winces!

I am, here, tacitly contrasting 'Literary Realism' with 'Melodrama', imputing to the former term a connotation of greater restraint and a finer-grained mode of mimesis, and the latter a more histrionic and more caricatured one. Alternatively 'realism' might be contrasted to 'idealism', in which the latter term speaks to a refusal to be bogged-down by merely material, quotidian concerns of the former.[7] To describe 'melodrama' as *histrionic* dallies, perhaps, with tautology, since a drama performed upon the stage is necessarily that; and it is a common enough assumption that the players in such on-stage dramas, like Mme Laure, carry away some of the heightened, self-dramatising and intensified being-in-the-world of their jobs into their private lives. *Middlemarch*, as a novel, certainly suggests so. That said, these two scales, realist-melodramatic and realist-idealist, themselves cross-over one another in unexpected ways.

Characterisation, in a novel as in a play or film, relies to a significant extent on the author's audience importing, and in some cases actively cathecting, their own priors (assumptions and desires or dislikes) into the wire-frame figure the author lays down. This co-creation is not entirely a free-for-all, of course; the specifics of the text provide guide rails, as do our broader contextual assumptions about human nature, social mores and so on. The point is that these contexts themselves exist in a relationship with the textual representations of those contexts, like novels. They are, indeed, nothing but textual. We might think of our own actual lived-experiences as 'realist', and might therefore consider 'melodrama' to be a mode that formally misconstrues 'reality'. But to put it in these terms is already to be complicit with a set of assumptions that *le naturalisme* has already framed in particular ways. We draw some of our beliefs about how we can and should act from our upbringing and our peer groups, and some we decide upon for ourselves, but we draw much also from the culture we consume. Indeed these three disciplines, or discourses, are all complexly interconnected.

Mme Laure and Dorothea, for instance, might seem very different individuals. The one kills her husband in plain view; the other is so intensely morally and spiritually scrupulous that such an action would

---

7   The entry on 'realism' in Raymond Williams's *Keywords: A Vocabulary of Culture and Society* (Oxford: Oxford University Press, 1976) remains, half a century after it was published, essential.

be perfectly inconceivable to her. The one, we might say, is *outré* and the other reticent, even repressed. Yet Eliot, it seems to me, goes out of her way to introduce an element into her textual creation of Dorothea that we can also describe as histrionic.

In Book 4 Dorothea, rebuffed yet again by the chill of her husband, and anxious for his health, becomes not tearful but angry:

> She was in the reaction of a rebellious anger stronger than any she had felt since her marriage. Instead of tears there came words:—
>
> 'What have I done—what am I—that he should treat me so? He never knows what is in my mind—he never cares. What is the use of anything I do? He wishes he had never married me.'[8]

This speech by Dorothea, and especially its latter part, falls into blank verse:

> What is the use of anything I do?
> He wishes he had never married me.

Two perfect iambic pentameters. Nor is this an isolated instance. Even if we confine ourselves to Book 4, it is remarkable to note how often Dorothea, alone of all Eliot's characters, speaks this way.[9]

But then perhaps it is only fitting that this happens with Dorothea, since she of all the main characters in the novel she is the one whose

---

8   Eliot, *Middlemarch*, ch. 42.
9   I do not claim that Dorothea always speaks in full pentameters; nor is every line that Eliot puts into her mouth entirely regular. But I do argue there is a distinct iambic pulse to the way she speaks that isn't the case for Eliot's other characters. Here, just from Book 4, are some examples of what I mean, from Dorothea's dialogue: 'I cannot bear to think that any one/Should die and leave no love behind' [ch. 34]; 'I've often thought that I should like to talk/To you again. It seems [most] strange to me/How many things I said to you.' [ch. 37]; '[...] I should have said/That those who have great thoughts get too much worn/In working [of] them out. I used to feel/About that, even [as] a little girl.' [ch. 37]; [Of Ladislaw's grandparents] 'I wonder how she bore the change from wealth/To poverty: I wonder whether she/Was happy with her husband! Do you know?' [ch. 37]; 'Ah, what a different life from mine! I have/Had always too much [here] of everything./But tell me how it was.' [ch. 37]; 'You must remember that you have not done/What he thought best for you. [...]/Perhaps my uncle has not told you how/Serious Mr. Casaubon's illness was./It would be very petty of us who/Are well and can bear things, to think much of/Small offences [...]' [ch. 37]; [speaking to Casaubon, regarding Ladislaw] 'I fear you think too hardly of him, dear./You are so good, so just—[and] you have done/Everything that you thought to be right.' [ch. 37]. Even when her speech doesn't fill-out into whole pentameters it's very often strongly iambic: 'I wish you could have stayed' [ch. 37]; 'Pray tell me what it is' [ch. 39] 'My life is very simple' [ch. 39].

self-conception tends to err on side of histrionism, that is, of conceiving herself not as a simple subjectivity but a figure playing a particular role—at the novel's opening, a spiritual or elevated role. Eliot is surely correct to intuit that such a self-conception includes a theatrical, self-dramatising component.

Dorothea's representation is a tension between what we might call 'melodrama' and a more restrained, diagnostic 'realism'. So is Lydgate's. But there is an important difference. Dorothea's desire to live a heightened rather than a mundane life—heightened according to a particular set of spiritual and scholarly criteria—is inherently self-dramatising, or so Eliot says. With Lydgate, by contrast, she separates out her character into a 'melodramatic' phase, disposed into his Parisian backstory, and a 'realist' phase, in which the character's very commitment to close medical and scientific observation mirrors the precise realist strategies Eliot herself deploys. This 'medical' scientific realism, this microscopic attentiveness to the somatic particular, also derives from Lydgate's Parisian backstory. But, this component of Lydgate's narrative weave grows in a different direction.

Cod-Shakespearian blank verse is not the only literary register deployed. The lyric that heads-up chapter 15, the portion of the novel that contains the story of Mme Laure, is one composed by Eliot herself:

> Black eyes you have left, you say,
> Blue eyes fail to draw you;
> Yet you seem more rapt to-day,
> Than of old we saw you.
>
> Oh, I track the fairest fair
> Through new haunts of pleasure;
> Footprints here and echoes there
> Guide me to my treasure:
>
> Lo! she turns—immortal youth
> Wrought to mortal stature,
> Fresh as starlight's aged truth—
> Many-named Nature!

The 'black eyes' connote tragic passion (Mme Laure) and the blue represent the more balanced and comedic possible woman (Rosamond, as Lydgate thinks). And indeed, this epigraph is saying that, at this stage in the story, Lydgate has turned away from both the dangerous passionate and the beautifully proper in favour of his scientific endeavours.

The poem is Eliot's, but the trope on which it is based—the choice faced by a (male) narrator between the intensity of a queenly 'black-eyed' lover and the calmer English rose represented by 'blue-eyes'— appears enough times in eighteenth- and nineteenth-century popular verse to render it almost a commonplace. Take for instance Alaric Watts, 'The Bachelor's Dilemma' (1823).[10] In this poem, the narrator is torn between loving Fanny 'whose form, like the willow, so slender and lithe/Has a thousand wild motions of lightness and grace' and her sister Helen 'more stately of gesture and mien,/Whose beauty a world of dark ringlets enshrouds/With a black, regal eye, and the step of a queen'.

> And when sorrow and joy are so blended together,
> That to weep I'm unwilling, to smile am as loth;
> When the beam may be kicked by the weight of a feather;
> I would fain keep it even—by wedding them both!
>
> But since I must fix or on black eyes or blue,
> Quickly make up my mind 'twixt a Grace and a Muse;
> Pr'ythee Venus, instruct me that course to pursue
> Which even Paris himself had been puzzled to choose!

The twist at the end of the poem is that the man asks for the hand of first one, then the other, and both turn him down, for 'lively Fanny declared he was somewhat too grave,/And Saint Helen pronounced him a little too gay!' The application is clear enough: light-heartedly in the case of the Watts poem, more complexly and with more serious emotional consequences in the case of Lydgate, the man who believes he has a free choice between two different modes of womanhood will find— surprise!—that he ends up with neither. In Lydgate's case, neither the promise of dark passion represented by Mme Laure, nor the fantasy of blue-eyed complaisance and comedy he thinks, at first, is Rosamond.

---

10 This poem was often reprinted and anthologised, and is here quoted from Alaric Alexander Watts, ed., *The Literary Souvenir, or, Cabinet of Poetry and Romance* (London: [n.p.], 1826), pp. 89–91. Watts was a very popular anthologist and writer in the Victorian period, and one we know that Eliot read: see for instance Avrom Fleishman, *George Eliot's Intellectual Life* (Cambridge: Cambridge University Press, 2010), p. 19, https://doi.org/10.1017/cbo9780511691706; William Baker and Donald P. Leinster-Mackay, *The Libraries of George Eliot and George Henry Lewes* (Victoria, BC: English Literary Studies, University of Victoria, 1981), p. 26.

More broadly, Watts's coyly glancing, comic hint at bigamy (his fantasy of 'wedding them both') becomes in Eliot's novel a sequential drama styling Dorothea's choice as serious, if never quite tragic. To the question *should she marry Casaubon or Ladislaw?* the novel provides the surprising answer: *both*. This is, of course, not an easy matter, and it costs Dorothea materially and socially to do it, but it nonetheless points to an attitude towards erotic choice that is all the more potent, even true-to-life, because it is counter-intuitive: that the choice is not between A and B, as we perhaps think, but rather between A + B and neither.

When Lydgate arrives in Middlemarch he is twenty-seven years old, 'an age', Eliot observes, 'at which many men are not quite common'. Not yet 'middle-aged' in Middlemarch, uncommon in a good as well as a more dubious sense. We are told he had studied medicine at Paris, and the novel makes the specific comparison between him and the French anatomist and physician Marie François Xavier Bichat:

> [...] about 1829 the dark territories of Pathology were a fine America for a spirited young adventurer. Lydgate was ambitious above all to contribute towards enlarging the scientific, rational basis of his profession. The more he became interested in special questions of disease, such as the nature of fever or fevers, the more keenly he felt the need for that fundamental knowledge of structure which just at the beginning of the century had been illuminated by the brief and glorious career of Bichat, who died when he was only one-and-thirty, but, like another Alexander, left a realm large enough for many heirs. That great Frenchman first carried out the conception that living bodies, fundamentally considered, are not associations of organs which can be understood by studying them first apart, and then as it were federally; but must be regarded as consisting of certain primary webs or tissues, out of which the various organs—brain, heart, lungs, and so on—are compacted.[11]

This might put us in mind of Gillian Beer's influential reading of *Middlemarch*'s realism as a distinctively post-Darwinian 'web of affinities'. As Beer notes, Eliot 'was often taken to task by contemporary reviewers

---

11   Eliot, *Middlemarch*, ch. 15. Eliot makes a rare misstep in her research here, for Bichat was thirty, not thirty-one when he died (he expired 22 July 1802; his birthday wasn't until November). It may be that Eliot had read this accurate but confusingly-phrased bit of Pierre Auguste Béclard's *Additions to the General Anatomy of Xavier Bichat* (Boston: Richardson and Lord, 1823), here translated by George Hayward: 'How many researches has BICHAT opened for us the way! What an immense inheritance he has left us to improve! Yet BICHAT died before he completed his thirty-second year', p. xv.

for the persistent scientific allusions in her works'.[12] The point is that, even on the most elementary level, we might complain that a scientist could not see—let us say—a beautiful woman in the way an artist could and should, and that it was the latter that readers wanted. There is a related issue where science is concerned, summed-up in the proverb about being unable to see the wood for the trees. Lydgate's great, hopeless ambition is, in one sense, the opposite of Casaubon's great, hopeless ambition: not a syncretic overview of everything, but a minute zeroing-in on the smallest element of which everything is made, that unit biologists and zoologists now recognise in genetic code and the building-blocks of cellular life. *Middlemarch*'s narrator ventriloquises Lydgate's philosophy:

> No man, one sees, can understand and estimate the entire structure or its parts—what are its frailties and what its repairs, without knowing the nature of the materials. [... Even Bichat] did not go beyond the consideration of the tissues as ultimate facts in the living organism, marking the limit of anatomical analysis; but it was open to another mind to say, have not these structures some common basis from which they have all started?[13]

'Of this sequence to Bichat's work' we are told 'Lydgate was enamoured [...] What was the primitive tissue?' This, I think, is the crucial point. If Casaubon is the novel's representative of textual, philological enquiry, and Ladislaw of political engagement, then Lydgate is Eliot's representative of science and the scientific approach. And from the first his ambition is *microscopic*. He aims small, on purpose. His final diminution into an affluent society doctor specialising in gout, is in a sense less his failure than it is the ironic consummation of his vision.

In this regard I part company with Beer's celebrated analysis of this novel. For her, Eliot's 'scientific' discourse, grounding as it does her specie of 'realism', is informed by two very large questions: throughout the novel, she says, 'two precepts are persisted presented, criticised, celebrated: "The power of nature is the power of motion" and "Evolution is the universal process".'[14] A contrary argument would repudiate such

---

12   Beer, *Darwin's Plots*, p. 149.

13   Eliot, *Middlemarch*, ch. 15.

14   Beer, *Darwin's Plots*, 155. She adds: 'the universality of both laws and their preoccupation not with replication but with change are seen as mutually confirmatory [...] in *Middlemarch* the historical aspect of both laws is expressed: individuals are trapped in the determined pace of successive historical moments.'

Casaubonic ambition as the 'key' to this novel, and suggest rather a much more granular, close-focus model of scientific 'realism' at work. Beer quotes a passage from *Daniel Deronda*:

> It was impossible to be jealous of Juliet Fenn, a girl as middling as mid-day market in everything but her archery and plainness, in which last she was noticeable like her father: underhung and with receding brow resembling that of the more intelligent fishes. (Surely, considering the importance which is given to such an accident in female offspring, marriageable men, or what the new English calls 'intending bridegrooms,' should look at themselves dispassionately in the glass, since their natural selection of a mate prettier than themselves is not certain to bar the effect of their own ugliness.)[15]

In this passage Beer rightly identifies a 'harsh, awkward tone', a 'faintly facetious, orotund style' that appears (she argues) when Eliot is 'driven by ideas that cause her deep disquiet and which she yet cannot repudiate'. But what applies to the rather darker *Deronda* does not, I think, fit *Middlemarch*'s less cut-throat world-picture.

This has more to do with the realism we associate with Balzac and Zola than the mode Eliot developed herself. The bustling sense of competition, the survival of the fittest, above all the overdetermined representation of Rougon-Macquart bloodlines by which character traits are directly passed down the generation and magnified, or enormified, across the years. It seems unfair to call Zola's immense, detailed textual canvases 'crude', and yet I am moved to suggest that there's nothing so heavy-handed as any of this in *Middlemarch*. And one reason for that is the way Eliot's scientific focus in this novel is not on evolutionary science—not on fossil hunters and palaeontology, naturalists or Lamarckians—but on Robert Brown's molecular jiggling and Lydgate's specifically somatic, medical ambitions.

Dan Rebellato contextualises Zola's medico-scientific realism in terms of Michel Foucault's *Birth of the Clinic*. Foucault posits the creation of a new 'medical gaze' across the eighteenth- and nineteenth-century, one that aims for a clarity so purified by science as to render the patient's body, and that body's implicature in its various matrices of relationships, invisible:

---

15 George Eliot, *Daniel Deronda* (Edinburgh: William Blackwood and Sons, 1876), http://www.gutenberg.org/files/7469/7469-h/7469-h.htm, ch. 11.

The dominant mode of medical practice at the start of that period was nosology, a classificatory approach to disease. Still very much in thrall to the Ancients, doctors relied on pre-existing taxonomies of disease connected by complex interrelations and hierarchies; consultations were a matter of establishing those symptoms that allowed the doctor to allocate the patient's illness within the established classificatory system. By the end of that period, the doctor is required purely to observe the patient without the intervention of theory or language. The body becomes a transparent vessel through which disease can be observed and thus eliminated. To use Zola's language, the nineteenth-century clinic was a means to show all so that all may be cured.[16]

The idea that we might, by seeing all (by taking in all that the writer has laid out for us to see) pass beyond the messy variegations of collective materiality into some rarified zone of transparency connects, it seems to me, much more resonantly with Eliot's than Zola's praxis.[17] *Middlemarch*, after all, is the novel prepared not only to close in, microscopically, on the mundaneness of ordinary human life, but to do so in order to invoke the Pascalian doubled-infinity 'hearing the grass grow and the squirrel's heart beat' beyond which is the transcendent, perhaps divine, 'roar which lies on the other side of silence'. [18]

Rebellato notes how Foucault's 'medical gaze' is 'constituted by a "double silence": the silence of theory and the silence of language'.[19] Critics have, I think, not paid enough attention to the valences of silence in *Middlemarch*—with the exception, perhaps, of the attention that has manifestly been bestowed upon this famous if, perhaps deliberately,

---

16 Rebellato, 'Sightlines', p. 149.

17 For a rather different reading of *Middlemarch* via Foucault, see Jeremy Tambling, '*Middlemarch*, Realism and the Birth of the Clinic', *ELH*, 57.4 (1990), 939–60.

18 Eliot, *Middlemarch*, ch. 20.

19 Rebellato, 'Sightlines', p. 153. He elucidates: 'By the silence of theory, Foucault means that nothing can intervene between the gaze and its object. Patterns may be found but they may not be looked for, for fear of imposing a prior structure on the gaze and its objects.' As for the second silence, the silence of language, this registers concerns that writing tends to 'introduces a spatial and temporal interval into the gaze. Speech is to be preferred as the immediate form in which the discoveries of the gaze can be communicated. Tis speech neutrally reproduces what is seen, in "a language that is the very speech of things [...] a language without words". This language is frictionless, silent, without remainder'. Rebellato's essay seeks to apply these insights to the realist theatre; my focus here, of course, is to explore the extent to which epigraphs and quotations, as nodes of embedded writing, figure disruptively *as* this deplored Foucauldian 'remainder'.

opaque reference to the roar that lies on its far side. Even just considering Lydgate, we see how Eliot combines the reticence and discretion we expect of our doctors, with Lydgate's habits of silence—tactful, or pusillanimous—in the face of his wife's dominance and her sometimes bad behaviour. There is also a silence in the novel with respect to his erotic choices. In saying so I am not just referring to the fact that, like any mainstream Victorian novelist, Eliot writes nothing sexually explicit. That much is obvious. What I mean is that Lydgate himself construes his own desire in terms of a reticence profound enough to prove, in the end, pathological.

In Chapter 16 Eliot writes the scene in which Lydgate falls for Rosamond, and in doing so positions his burgeoning desire in relation not only to the melodramatic past of Mme Laure and Paris, but in terms of a slyly critiqued 'normative' model of nineteenth-century feminine allure:

> Lydgate was almost forgetting that he must carry on the conversation, in thinking how lovely this creature was, her garment seeming to be made out of the faintest blue sky, herself so immaculately blond, as if the petals of some gigantic flower had just opened and disclosed her; and yet with this infantine blondness showing so much ready, self-possessed grace. Since he had had the memory of Laure, Lydgate had lost all taste for large-eyed silence: the divine cow no longer attracted him, and Rosamond was her very opposite.[20]

Divine cow strikes us, perhaps, as a less than flattering way of referring to feminine allure; still, we have to read the whole novel fully to understand that the 'large-eyed silence' mentioned here contains more than mere feminine delicacy or reticence—to begin to understand, that is, what manner of roar is reputed to lie on the far side of it. The pursuit of such noise does indeed prove fatal first to Lydgate's self-esteem and finally to him as a person.

Book 6 is called 'The Widow and the Wife'—which is to say, Dorothea and Rosamond. In chapter 58 Rosamond wants to go riding. Her husband forbids her, on account of her pregnancy, because he (as a doctor as much as a spouse) considers the risk too great to their unborn child. She goes riding anyway, disobeying her husband. The horse bolts (startled by 'the crash of a tree that was being felled on the edge of

---

20   Eliot, *Middlemarch*, ch. 16.

Halsell wood') which causes 'a worse fright to Rosamond' which terror 'leads finally to the loss of her baby'. All the baby paraphernalia, 'all the embroidered robes and caps' have to be 'laid by in darkness'.

This is, we might say, a sad, even a tragic interlude in the story. But although Lydgate *is* saddened he is too decent to play the 'I told you so' game with his wife ('Lydgate could not show his anger towards her')—another iteration of Lydgatean silence. And the whole experience proves water off a duck's back for Rosamond herself: 'Rosamond was soon looking lovelier than ever at her worktable, enjoying drives in her father's phaeton and thinking it likely that she might be invited to Quallingham. She knew that she was a much more exquisite ornament to the drawing-room there than any daughter of the family'.

The episode illustrates not just that Rosamond is stubborn. It says something about the *nature* of her stubbornness. Her desire to go riding, against her husband's wishes, is connected with her desire to spend time with Lydgate's cousin, 'the Captain', who lacks Tertius's cleverness or moral purpose but is considerably more aristocratic and suave. Finding out about a first, illicit but uneventful, ride in the company of the Captain, Lydgate is angry, and declares he will speak to the man. Rosamond is not happy at this.

> 'I shall tell the Captain that he ought to have known better than offer you his horse,' he said, as he moved away.
>
> 'I beg you will not do anything of the kind, Tertius,' said Rosamond, looking at him with something more marked than usual in her speech. 'It will be treating me as if I were a child. Promise that you will leave the subject to me.'
>
> There did seem to be some truth in her objection. Lydgate said, 'Very well,' with a surly obedience, and thus the discussion ended with his promising Rosamond, and not with her promising him.
>
> In fact, she had been determined not to promise. Rosamond had that victorious obstinacy which never wastes its energy in impetuous resistance. What she liked to do was to her the right thing, and all her cleverness was directed to getting the means of doing it. She meant to go out riding again on the grey, and she did go on the next opportunity of her husband's absence, not intending that he should know until it was late enough not to signify to her.[21]

---

21 Eliot, *Middlemarch*, ch. 58.

It is a pinch-point in how we relate to this novel. We could put it this way, via two observations with which it is hard, I think, to demur. One is that a good proportion of Eliot's original readers in the 1870s would have read this chapter through a frame of beliefs that said, in effect: a wife should always obey her husband's commands, that he stands in relation to her as the head to the body and so on. Such an ideological frame will tend to make this episode a cautionary tale about what happens when a wife disobeys the proper authority of her spouse. But the second observation is that we, twenty-first-century readers, no longer tend to see marriage that way. We now believe that husband and wife are partners and see no inherent superiority in the man over the woman— indeed, belief in such notional superiority is called 'sexism' and is to be deplored. When Rosamond says that Lydgate's attempt to extract a promise from her not to go riding again is 'treating her like a child' she is—surely—*right*, isn't she? As a grown woman she ought to be able to decide what she does with her time. What about her decision that the ride had nothing to do with her miscarriage? ('Rosamond was mildly certain that the ride had made no difference, and that if she had stayed at home the same symptoms would have come on and would have ended in the same way, because she had felt something like them before'). Is this the heartless self-justification of a profoundly selfish, shallow and narcissistic individual, to be deplored because the 'proper' reaction to this event ought to be her learning to be less self-centred (which is to say her listening to, and obeying, her husband)? Or does she *have a point*? Miscarriage is a serious and distressing matter, and I have no desire to trivialise it, but: 'being scared by a horse' is, really, not a terribly plausible rationale for it. Had Rosamond *fallen* from her horse, it is possible a bad-enough impact might have resulted in miscarriage, but fright on its own is not a physiologically likely explanation for what happened.[22]

While I appreciate that I may be making slightly heavy weather of my point here, this is due to my uncertainty in how to read this episode in *Middlemarch*. The first time I encountered this section of the novel, many years ago, I had an almost visceral reaction against Rosamond. She struck me as a kind of monster of self-centredness, with a near sociopathic disregard for the feelings of others. Re-reading it more recently that reaction is still there, I suppose, but in a more compromised

---

22   See, e.g., https://www.nhs.uk/conditions/miscarriage/causes/.

and complicated way. I'm struck, for instance, how much our reaction to the episode is orchestrated to align our response with Lydgate's:

> Lydgate could only say, 'Poor, poor darling!'—but he secretly wondered over the terrible tenacity of this mild creature. There was gathering within him an amazed sense of his powerlessness over Rosamond.

Would it be possible, I wonder, to pull together a reading of the whole thing from Rosamond's point of view, to see some *admirable* in her tenacity (which only becomes 'terrible', surely, from a narrowly masculinist point of view, when it refuses to subordinate itself to the priorities of Lydgate)? To see the canniness with which she manipulates her marital situation so as to get her own way without occasioning a big stand-up row as, in a way, even creditable? Or is she just the monster of selfishness many readers take her to be? Dorothea works assiduously to subordinate her intellect and individuality to the needs of her husband, and look what that gets her. Yet we think of Dorothea as the 'heroine' of *Middlemarch*. What would a reading look like that put Rosamond in that role, I wonder?

I float this notion, though tentatively and without much force. Piecing together the various details Eliot construes with respect to Rosamond is liable only to convince us of how her energy and wilfulness are only ever put in service of herself. Earlier in the novel Eliot has Rosamond 'thinking that it was not so very melancholy to be mistress of Lowick Manor with a husband likely to die soon';[23] a pretty heartless and materialist mode of empathising with Dorothea's position. It might be that my concern, here, is less with the superficiality of Rosamond's characterisation than with the idea that *Middlemarch* contains a character rendered only in term of its superficies. That if we put Rosamond under our metaphorical microscope, we wouldn't see more granular psychological detail and specificity come into focus.

I have travelled some distance from this chapter's starting point, and should return to it before I conclude. Lydgate's microscopy, in this novel, carries with it something of a flavour of irony. We can agree with Eliot that, however skilled a scientist Lydgate might be at anatomising human beings, there are crucial aspects of humanity invisible to even the most powerful microscope. Lydgate might observe a person down to the level of the cell, but not see (as it might be) his wife's true nature, or the nature

---

23   Eliot, *Middlemarch*, ch. 31.

of love, or indeed the right way to organise one's time and will to achieve one's scientific goals. That looks a little like a cheap shot—it is in fact, a point both facile and obvious—but it has a larger resonance. Why, Eliot is tacitly saying, should a novelist, even one so clever and insightful as Marian Evans, be any better at analysing human beings than Lydgate? Isn't he as learned, as clever? His instrument, the microscope, is one that zeroes-in on minutiae, but does Eliot's lens not do the same?

Catherine Jackson has shown how the exact period Eliot is writing about saw a series of linked advanced in glass-blowing, that 'between about 1825 and 1835' resulted in glass being used 'in distinctly new ways', with particular consequences for developments in chemistry.[24] This is another way in which Eliot, in *Middlemarch*, is being preternaturally attentive to the actual historical context of her imagined world. Isobel Armstrong notes how often, in the nineteenth-century, 'the microscope and the telescope (each with different histories) were frequently described as forming a perfect antithesis', before demurring:

> Their objects of study are not comparable, however: far distant bodies in motion seen by the light of prehistory, sub-visible entities, dissected into infinitesimal sections or pullulating with importunate life in a drop of water. Extreme nearness and endless particulars, not the dissolving view, are the microscopes essence.[25]

Middlemarch finds middle way, fittingly, between 'extreme nearness and endless particulars' on the one hand, and a mistier 'dissolving view' on the other. But what Armstrong goes on to talk about is the inherently conflicted nature of the glasswork that constituted these microscopic lenses.

> Moreover [microscopy] was incorporated into glass culture with a degree of popular epistemophilia and scopic wonder quite unlike popular accounts of the telescope. Nevertheless, though for very different reasons, the microscope created the ungrounded perspectival world that emerged in astronomy and spectacle alike. Its structural

---

24 Catherine M. Jackson, 'The "Wonderful Properties of Glass": Liebig's Kaliapparat and the Practice of Chemistry in Glass', *Isis*, 106.1 (2015), 43–69, https://doi.org/10.1086/681036

25 Isobel Armstrong, *Victorian Glassworlds: Glass Culture and the Imagination 1830–1880* (Oxford: Oxford University Press, 2008), p. 301. See also Mark Wormald, 'Microscopy and Semiotic in *Middlemarch*', *Nineteenth-Century Literature*, 50 (1996), 501–24, https://doi.org/10.2307/2933926

refraction organizes all its images. Additionally, under the microscope at this time, the object exists in atopic space, preternaturally distinct, but freed from relational coordinates. It has no norms. As Catherine Wilson has pointed out, one image is predicated on losing another. The image is like a metonomy where the referential term has been amputated.

This ought to remind us of the passage previously quoted from Pascal, and the way *Middlemarch* 'middles' us as readers between the very small and the very large. Lawrence Rothfield locates Lydgate's microscopy in a particular medical discursive context, the 'long, arduous' task of 'integrating cell theory into medical science', something only 'finally accomplished during the latter half of the century'.

> During the interim, medicine had to continue, even though a fissure began to open up between cellular and human life, between the innumerable activities of individual cells and the fluent progression of a disease through the tissues of the body, between the microscopic and macroscopic constituents of the self.[26]

For Rothfield, this 'divergence of pathology from other organismic sciences' presented as a problem, to which 'Lydgate's predicament, and more generally, *Middlemarch* as a whole, stands as a kind of response, or more accurately, an accommodation'.[27] My argument is rather different, more metatextual and reflexive; that Eliot is knowingly pitching her novel between the infinities of smallness gestured at by microscopy and the frightening Pascalian infinities of vastness opened-up by telescopy. And, more to the point, it is that the lenses slotted into the eyepiece are epigraphic and quotational, small forms that open when the eye is properly applied to them, into compelling and open-ended new vistas. In textual terms the epigraph is small and the novel is large, and in terms of the relationship between art and life the former is small and the latter vast; but in both (interrelated) situations there is something uniquely eloquent and potent inherent in the relationship *between* these smallnesses and these largenesses. In that middle.

---

26 Rothfield, *Vital Signs*, p. 97.
27 Ibid., p. 99. His argument is that this disparity figures Eliot's larger social vision: 'if, as seems to be the case, medicine and cell theory really are incommensurable sciences, different species of discourse yielding unreconciled versions of the truth about the same object—the body—then the Comteian ideal of a social order crowned and informed by scientific order (an ideal cherished by Eliot and many of her contemporaries) may be compromised'.

4. Hypocrisy and
the Judgment of Men

The middleness of *Middlemarch* is a moral as well as an existential quantity, a matter of ethics as both mediated and medial. The novel's twinned mirrors situate questions of honesty or mendacity, and Eliot's characters middle themselves somewhere between moral puritanism on the one hand—Dorothea's over-identification with St Theresa, or Antigone, we might say—and active malignancy on the other (the melodramatic blackmailing villainy of John Raffles, say). And this brings me to another epigraph.

At the head of chapter 38 we read: 'C'est beaucoup que le jugement des hommes sur les actions humaines; tôt ou tard il devient efficace'. This means: 'the judgement of men on human affairs is a serious business; sooner or later it always comes into force'. Eliot identifies the line's provenance: 'Guizot'—that is, the French historian François Pierre Guillaume Guizot. It is worth taking the trouble to locate the original context for this quotation in Guizot's 1835 *Course in Modern History*, part of his discussion of the Middle Ages, an epoch in which he diagnoses a kind of radical hypocrisy. Medieval people, Guizot argues, possessed genuinely-held high and spiritual ideals, and yet nonetheless lived lives of remarkable brutality and venality. How to reconcile this seeming contradiction?

> *Mais quelle que soit la cause, le fait est indubitable. On le rencontre partout au moyen âge, dans les poésies populaires comme dans les exhortations des prêtres. Partout la pensée morale des hommes s'élève et aspire fort au-dessus de leur vie. Et gardez-vous de croire que, parce qu'elle ne gouvernait pas immédiatement les actions, parce que la pratique démentait sans cesse et étrangement la théorie, l'influence de la théorie fût nulle et sans valeur. C'est beaucoup que le jugement des hommes sur les actions humaines; tôt ou tard il devient efficace. 'J'aime*

  https://doi.org/10.11647/OBP.0249.04

COURS

D'HISTOIRE

MODERNE,

PAR M. GUIZOT,

PROFESSEUR D'HISTOIRE A LA FACULTÉ DES LETTRES DE PARIS.

HISTOIRE

DE LA CIVILISATION EN FRANCE,

DEPUIS LA CHUTE DE L'EMPIRE ROMAIN,
JUSQU'EN 1789.

TOME I.

Bruxelles,

LOUIS HAUMAN ET COMPAGNIE.

1835

Fig. 3 François Pierre Guillaume Guizot, *Cours D'Histoire Moderne* (Brussels: Louis Hauman & Co., 1835), vol. 1, title page, https://www.google.co.uk/books/edition/_/aYNfDbifZJoC?hl=en&gbpv=1. Public domain.

mieux une mauvaise action qu'un mauvais principe', dit quelque part Rousseau, et Rousseau avait raison.[1]

But whatever the cause, the facts cannot be denied. This phenomenon is found everywhere in the Middle Ages, as much in popular poetry as in the exhortations of the priests. Everywhere the moral thought of men rises and aspires far above their mundane lives. But don't be fooled into believing—because it didn't directly inform their actions, because their practice was continually at odds with their theory—that this influence was nothing, or had no value. The judgment of men on human actions is a serious matter, and, sooner or later, it always takes effect: 'I prefer a bad action to a bad principle', says Rousseau somewhere, and Rousseau is right.

This larger context is particularly interesting, speaking as it does to the novel as a moral as well as a physical middling: a commitment to

---

1   François-Pierre Guillaume Guizot, *Cours D'Histoire Moderne: Histoire de la Civilisation en France* (Paris: Didier, 1846), vol. 3, pp. 363–4, https://www.google.co.uk/books/edition/Histoire_de_la_civilisation_en_France/_A-HYbpWLgQC?hl=en&gbpv=1

compromise and an acceptance of people as themselves always to one degree or another morally compromised.

When Bulstrode's story eventually unwinds he becomes, I would argue, less an object of readerly contumely than of readerly sympathy, not despite but because of the exposure his earlier altitudes of Methodist hypocrisy. 'There may be coarse hypocrites, who consciously affect beliefs and emotions for the sake of gulling the world', is how Eliot puts it; 'but Bulstrode was not one of them. He was simply a man whose desires had been stronger than his theoretic beliefs, and who had gradually explained the gratification of his desires into satisfactory agreement with those beliefs. If this be hypocrisy, it is a process which shows itself occasionally in us all, to whatever confession we belong. There is no general doctrine which is not capable of eating out our morality if unchecked by the deep-seated habit of direct fellow-feeling with individual fellow-men'.[2] Like Rousseau, Eliot prefers bad actions to bad 'doctrine'. Like him, I'd say, she is right.

Chapter 38 itself is given over to a quartet of Middlemarchian eminences. To begin with, the Cadwalladers and Sir James Chettam discuss the political situation, deploring Ladislaw's editorship of the *Pioneer* and the potential for radical political upheaval they believe this represents. They are joined later in the chapter by Mr. Brooke, who argues the contrary case, in favour of political reform. This party embodies two different valences of, more or less, *political* hypocrisy. 'I do wish people would behave like gentlemen', is Sir James's essential-oil-of-Toryism ('feeling', Eliot nicely glosses her character's statement 'that this was a simple and comprehensive programme for social wellbeing'). 'Behaving like a gentleman' is, it seems, a capacious enough political programme to encompass both nobility *and* venality.

> 'I thought the most expensive hobby in the world was standing for Parliament,' said Mrs. Cadwallader. 'They said the last unsuccessful candidate at Middlemarch—Giles, wasn't his name?—spent ten thousand pounds and failed because he did not bribe enough. What a bitter reflection for a man!'
>
> 'Somebody was saying,' said the Rector, laughingly, 'that East Retford was nothing to Middlemarch, for bribery.'

---

2   Eliot, *Middlemarch*, ch. 61.

> 'Nothing of the kind,' said Mr. Brooke. 'The Tories bribe, you know: Hawley and his set bribe with treating, hot codlings, and that sort of thing; and they bring the voters drunk to the poll. But they are not going to have it their own way in future—not in future, you know. Middlemarch is a little backward, I admit—the freemen are a little backward. But we shall educate them—we shall bring them on, you know. The best people there are on our side.'[3]

The issue is not bribery as such, but only the most effective modes of applying inducements to the electorate to obtain one's political preference. Brooke's Liberalism only *seems* more idealistic and less hypocritical than Sir James's Toryism. In fact, his unfittedness for political office is embodied in his small-scale incompetence and various abdications as a landlord, all satirised in Ladislaw's paper.

Hannah Arendt thought that 'hypocrisy is the vice of vices', because 'integrity can indeed exist under the cover of all other vices except this one. Only crime and the criminal, it is true, confront us with the perplexity of radical evil; but only the hypocrite is really rotten to the core'.[4] But Eliot doesn't really believe anyone is rotten *to the core*, and whilst she is of course not *endorsing* hypocrisy in this novel she is nonetheless reflecting on the extent to which the various compromises humans end-up making with absolute virtue, absolute duty and the noblest aims 'middle' us all in the reality of social existence. Very medieval, in Guizotian terms, we might think. Not for nothing is that period called the 'middle' ages.

There are other ways in which we might conceptualise what could be called hypocrisy. There is, for instance, Robert Browning's celebrated insistence that a man's reach should exceed his grasp (or what's a heaven for?), the gap between reach and aim emblematising this very term. True, if we reach for something beyond our grasp unknowingly, an instinctive or unaware over-reaching, we probably wouldn't use the word 'hypocrisy'; but I wonder whether what Browning is saying is something more profound, that we not only do but should *knowingly* over-reach ourselves, that we should enact a kind of disingenuousness about what we can achieve, what can be achieved. This, it seems to me, is closer to hypocrisy, albeit one that Browning styles as a paradoxically divine one.

---

3   Ibid., ch. 38.
4   Hannah Arendt, *On Revolution* (Harmondsworth: Penguin Books, 1990), p. 103.

One person's hypocrisy might be another's realism; it might be spun as honesty in a system one considers weighted *against* honesty and truthfulness. The problem with this view is that it describes all systems. Civilisation, as Freud so persuasively argues, necessarily entails its discontents; hypocrisy could be thought part of the needful superstructuring of the latter so as to maintain the former—the tribute, as the old phrase has it, vice pays to virtue. This is particularly true in the magisterium of politics, 'particularly true' in the sense that we all recognise that politicians are especially prone to hypocrisy. David Runciman has insightfully explored the way 'politics' is a combination of more-or-less calcified ritual and ceremony on the one hand, and pragmatic horse-trading on the other, such that the latter will in actual political life tend to hide behind the former. 'Politics requires us to talk about complex issues as though they were simple, and to keep hidden from public view some of the nastier deals and compromises that enable us to get things done in communities made up of millions of quarrelsome, naive and opinionated people'.[5] Isn't this also the (to fall into cliché for a moment) 'journey' Dorothea goes on?—*from* an unworldly idealism that proves harmful to her and others, *towards* a wiser comprehension of how the world, and love, actually works, and the compromises one must make with both. Or is this to confuse our broader tolerance for 'hypocrisy' in a specifically 'party political' context with the ways hypocrisy manifests in our emotional and spiritual lives? Bulstrode is revealed to be a whited sepulchre; but he also committed criminal acts and was implicated in a man's death. This is more than the common-garden hypocrisies that delineate our ordinary, sublunary humanity. Is it hypocritical, in any sense, for Casaubon to believe Dorothea could love him? Or that he could control her after his death? Is Fred Vincy a hypocrite for allowing his easy-going preference for pleasure to interfere with his sterner interpersonal duty? Hypocrisy seems the wrong word in this context. It's the flipside of the Browning quotation I mention above. The English word derives etymologically from the

---

5   David Runciman, *Political Hypocrisy: The Mask of Power, from Hobbes to Orwell and Beyond* (Princeton: Princeton University Press, 2010), p. 130. Runciman makes a distinction between this kind of 'first order' hypocrisy, which he thinks is baked-into the political process, and what he calls 'second order' hypocrisy, in which politicians cynically exploit the public's sense that a double-standard applies. He deplores this second kind of hypocrisy.

Ancient Greek ὑπόκρισις, which means 'answer, stage acting, pretence', coming out of the broader discourse of theatrical performance. When we reach for something we know is beyond our grasp, we are *performing* the action, even if only for our own benefit, in the sense that being aware our gesture is futile does not prompt us to the honesty of giving up. We could go further and suggest: life, actually, is stitched-together out of such moments, such gestures, such forlorn hopes, essays into action, gambles on relationships, on work, on hope itself.

The epigraph to chapter 10 is a quotation from Thomas Fuller:

> 'He had catch'd a great cold, had he had no other clothes to wear than those of a skin of a Bear not yet killed.'—FULLER

This trims the actual quotation (from Fuller's 1662 *History of the Worthies of England*) a little: 'But he had catch'd a great cold, had he had no other clothes to wear then [*sic*] those which were to be made of a skin of a Bear not yet killed'.[6] The fuller sentence makes the sense clearer: Fuller describes someone in pressing need of clothes whose only option is a bearskin still on the outside of a live bear. The position of someone, in other words, who has a good deal of dangerous work to undertake before his necessity can be addressed.

Chapter 10 concerns Casaubon anticipating his impending marriage, and also records a dinner party in which various other Middlemarchians discuss the match. The application of the Fuller line to such a chapter is a little unclear. Does it refer to Ladislaw, whom (we are told in the opening paragraph) has left Middlemarch for Europe, with the implication that his nascent love for Dorothea has a long and arduous route to traverse, obstacles to overcome—her marriage to Casaubon—before it finds its consummation? Or does it refer to Casaubon? This is a character whom Eliot describes here, with nicely sensitive insight, as a man aware that he *ought* to be happy that he is going to marry this beautiful and attentive young woman who is nonetheless puzzled that he still experiences 'a certain blankness of sensibility' on the subject. Is his marital happiness his unskinned bear? Or does the epigraph relate to the later portion of the chapter, given over to Mr. Brooke's dinner party attended by Lady Chettham, Lydgate, Vincy, Bulstrode and others?

---

6   Thomas Fuller, *The History of the Worthies of England* [1662], ed. by John Nichols (London: F.C. and J. Rivington, 1811), vol. 1, p. 208.

We need a wider context. The line comes at the end of Fuller's entry on 'Mount-Edgecombe' (now spelled 'Mount Edgecumbe') in Cornwall:

MOUNT-EDGECOMBE. It was built by Sir Richard Edgecombe, Knight [...] In the Raign of Queen Mary (about the year 1555) he gave entertainment at one time, for some good space, to the Admirals of the English, Spanish, and Netherland, and many Noble-men besides. Mount Edgcombe was the scene of this Hospitality; a house new built and named by the aforesaid Knight, a square Structure with a round Turret at each end, garretted on the top. The Hall (rising above the rest) yieldeth a stately sound as one entereth it; the Parlour and Dyning-roome afford a large and diversified prospect both of Sea and Land. The high scituation (cool in Summer, yet not cold in Winter) giveth *health*: the neighbour River *wealth*: two Block-houses great safety: and the Town of Plymouth good company unto it. Nor must I forget the fruitful ground about it (pleasure without profit is but a Hower without a root); stored with Wood, Timber, Fruit, Deer, and Connies, a sufficiency of Pasture, Arable, and Meadow, with Stone, Lime, Marl, and what not.

I write not this to tempt the Reader to the breach of the Tenth Commandement, 'covet his Neighbour's house'; and one line in the prevention thereof: I have been credibly informed that the Duke of Medina Sidonia, Admiral of the Spanish Fleet in the year 88, was so affected at the *sight* of this House (though but beholding it at a distance, from the Sea) that he resolved it for his own possession in the partage of this Kingdome (blame him not if choosing best for himself), which they had pre-conquered in their hopes and expectation. But he had catch'd a great cold, had he had no other clothes to wear then those which were to be made of a skin of a Bear not yet killed.[7]

The whole passage contextualises Eliot's line as being not about an arduous road to eventual consummation, but, on the contrary, as a quasi-proverbial expression for desiring a manifest impossibility. The Duke of Medina Sidonia never did get his hands on Mount Edgecumbe, after all. So perhaps the focus of the epigraph is Dorothea herself—ironically so, in the sense that she does come into wifely possession of a fine house. Such a (material) thing was never Dorothea's goal, of course; she hoped for something more refined, spiritual and scholarly, but that—Eliot is saying—is like the Spanish Duke lusting after this English stately home.

The epigraph, in other words, is in its diffident way saying something large and profound, something with a pressing relevance to the novel.

---

7   Ibid.

It is saying that we cannot free our looking-forward from the shape that our desires (conscious or unconscious) give to our anticipations, from the taint of hypocrisy; because such desiring, by being future-orientated, becomes inevitably defined by the inconsiderable. Praxis will subvene upon eros.

This is especially the case for Dorothea because her desire is unsimple—as our desire so often is. She does not (as it might be) simply desire Casaubon; she desires something larger than Casaubon, and believes—her heart believes, at any rate—that he is the route to reaching it. In the words of Patricia McKee 'Dorothea's desire is not a desire to be met but a desire to be exceeded by something larger than herself'.[8] Her desire is at once a knowledge of her smallness and her ambition for greatness. Her desire, in other words, mediates not animal satisfactions nor social or material cupidity, but rather precisely the relation between the small and the large, between motto and majority.

We stand, small epigraphs, at the head of a large body of unread text—our future. Only when we have apprehended the latter will our relation to it, direct or ironic, clear or complex, become evident to us. That's what it means to exist in time. It may be that our desire, like Rosamond, or Fred Vincy, is only for material comfort and status—a lovely house, say—but, Eliot's novel suggests, this is not only subject to the vagaries, and so obliged to pay the price, of futurity as such; it also tangles us in more than we think. It gives us, whether we like it or not, skin in the game, bearish or other. What we end up doing in pursuit of such desire might be less than optimal: might be selfish, or bring suffering to others, or put them in financial danger, or ostracise them. It is not that bad actions are defensible as such; rather, it is just (Eliot is saying) that she prefers a bad action to a bad principle. And Eliot is right.

---

8   Patricia McKee, *Heroic Commitment in Richardson, Eliot, and James* (Princeton: Princeton University Press, 1986), p. 151.

5. Ladislaw

It is up to us, as readers, how we choose to pronounce Will Ladislaw's surname. We might assume that it rhymes its final syllable with 'coleslaw.' Then again, we could note the clues as to his family provenance that unobtrusively accumulate as the novel proceeds (starting in chapter 8, when Mr. Cadwallader explains Ladislaw's relationship to Casaubon: 'his mother's sister made a bad match—a Pole, I think—lost herself—at any rate was disowned by her family') and conclude that Will's name must actually be 'Wilhelm Ladisław'. He has presumably Englished his Christian name, and it is possible the English 'coleslaw' pronunciation of 'Ladislaw' is the one the book's characters use: we're in England after all, not Poland (the novel is *Middlemarch*, not *Centralnynaród*). But we cannot be sure, because Eliot's novel doesn't include a pronunciation guide. We can call Will 'Ladislāw' or 'Ladisclăv' depending on our preferences.

Eliot does not go out of her way to draw attention to Will's Polishness, but neither does she conceal it, and in a novel like *Middlemarch*, which is centrally and persistently about how we 'read' other people, how much nuance and insight (or blindness) there can be in such human reading, and how much our insights can be compromised by our prejudices, our inertia or our fantasies—in such a novel these questions are of course much more important than they might be in a different kind of fiction. All we know of Will by the end of Book One is: he's handsome, artistic, charming and something of an outsider. As the novel goes on we learn more. Making Will Polish makes him 'Romantic' in more senses than one.

This was because of the status of Poland in the early decades of the nineteenth-century. In 1788 the Polish king Stanisław II oversaw a new reformist national constitution. The country's neighbours, Russia and Prussia, fearing that the success of Stanisław's liberalising revolution

 https://doi.org/10.11647/OBP.0249.05

might destabilise their respective autocracies, carved the place up between them. In 1793, after a short war, independent Poland ceased to exist and the country was partitioned, with Russia and Prussia taking the lion's share and Austria acquiring some territory in the south. As you might expect Poles were not happy with this arrangement. There were several uprisings, some very bloody, throughout the nineteenth century, although in fact 'Poland' was not to exist again as a distinct nation until the twentieth century.

The political situation meant that other European countries, not least Britain, became home to many exiled Polish revolutionaries. Perhaps Ladislaw's grandfather fled from the initial war and partition (it is not spelled-out in the novel). What's undeniable is that during the timeline of *Middlemarch* 'Poland' was in the grip of by another upheaval, the 1830 'November Uprising'.

For many, and especially for younger Britons with radical or revolutionary sympathies, this uprising became a supremely Romantic symbol of doomed struggle against tyranny. Alfred Tennyson, twenty-one years old in 1830, took to dressing in the style associated with Polish exiles: a dark cloak and wide-brimmed floppy hat (he was still dressing that way in the 1890s). He wrote an epic poem about the nation's fate: 'a beautiful poem on Poland', he later told his friend William Allingham, 'hundreds of lines long—but the housemaid lit the fire with it. I never could recover it'[1] (other early Tennysonian poems celebrating the romantic dash of Polish resurrection do survive, including 1820's 'On the Late Russian Invasion of Poland').

The situation had not resolved itself, four decades later, when Eliot was writing her novel. A year before she began publishing *Middlemarch* Jules Verne published his submarine science-fiction novel *Twenty Thousand Leagues Under the Sea* (1870), in which a mysterious nobleman going by the name of 'Nemo' (that is, 'Nobody') uses his advanced submarine to make war on imperialism. In the original draft of his novel, Verne revealed at the end that Nemo was a Polish aristocrat taking revenge for Tsarist atrocities in his homeland. But Verne's publisher, Hetzel, conscious of how many copies of Verne's novels were sold in Russia (where much of the reading public spoke French), persuaded

---

1   Quoted in Norman Page (ed), *Tennyson: Interviews and Recollections* (London: Macmillan 1983), p. 141

him to change this to something less controversial, and Verne removed all specific references to Poland from the work—indeed, in *Twenty Thousand Leagues Under the Sea*'s sequel, *The Mysterious Island* (1875) 'Nemo' is revealed to be an Indian Prince with an animus against the British Empire.

As Tatiana Kuzmic points out:

> The 'Polish fever' that swept England in the 1830s reached such a pitch that beggars from other countries craftily exploited the nation's sympathies and, counting especially on the romantic fantasies of the 'fair sex,' managed to obtain money and lodgings by passing themselves off as impoverished Polish princes. Andrew Halliday, writing in the 1862 supplemental volume of Henry Mayhew's *London Labour and the London Poor* (1851), recalled these events in a section on 'Foreign Beggars,' and warned his audience that 'it will not do to mistake every vagabond refugee for a noble exile.' 'To be a Pole, and in distress, was almost a sufficient introduction,' Halliday stated, as well as 'so excellent an opportunity for that class of foreign swindlers which haunt roulette-tables, and are the pest of second-rate hotels abroad'.[2]

Will isn't quite in this position. He's no beggar, and he has his older cousin Casaubon to vouch for him. But some in Middlemarch regard him with a suspicion tainted with this kind of assumption: a handsome but indigent 'foreigner' working on the romantic fantasies of the 'fair sex' to obtain money.

Eliot knows exactly what she's doing by introducing this sort-of English, sort-of Polish character into the novel in the way she does. 'Ladislaw' is not an English surname, but then neither is 'Casaubon'—the famous Renaissance classical scholar Isaac Casaubon was a Huguenot exile in Switzerland. Eliot never makes explicit in *Middlemarch* if Edward is a scion of this notable family, but we can deduce from his surname that his roots are Huguenot—that is, that his ancestors were French Protestants who fled from Catholic France to Protestant Britain after the Saint Bartholomew's Massacre. Centuries separate them, but both Casaubon's and Ladislaw's forebears were refugees. That key theme of *Middlemarch* is, alas, as relevant in our twenty-first-century world as it has ever been. The creeping prejudice by which people who self-identify

---

2   Tatiana Kuzmic, '"The German, the Sclave, and the Semite": Eastern Europe in the Imagination of George Eliot', *Nineteenth-Century Literature*, 68.4 (2014), 513–41 (p. 519), https://doi.org/10.1525/ncl.2014.68.4.513

as 'English' view Polish people on British streets with suspicion or hostility could hardly, as of the 2020s, be more current.

There is a difference, though, in the refugee ancestry of Casaubon and Ladislaw, even though the two men are connected by blood. Huguenots were refugees from specifically religious persecution; the Polish diaspora of the nineteenth-century were political refugees. And Eliot, carefully if unobtrusively, explores the consonances and differences of these two modes of exile as her novel goes on. It gives us, for example, one of the ways in which we can parse Dorothea's dilemma: the theologian versus the politician, or if not quite that, the man dedicated to the theological and mythological past, and the man engaged in shaping the political and social future. That this dilemma is also construed in terms of an unattractive older man—dead (it seems) from the waist down—and a sexually compelling younger man is not arbitrary, although it perhaps doesn't quite amount to Eliot's thumb in the balance. But in addition to interpellating us, as readers, into Dorothea's situation, it becomes another way in which *Middlemarch* engages its relationship to epigraphy and quotation—to, that is, tradition and novelty. The dynamic is straightforwardly established early on. It is Mr. Brooke, hardly the most politically engaged of Eliot's characters, who says to Casaubon, 'smiling towards' him: 'I remember when we were all reading Adam Smith. There is a book, now. I took in all the new ideas at one time—human perfectibility, now'. His conclusion ('we must have Thought; else we shall be landed back in the dark ages') constellates thought as such and novelty, and he adds 'But talking of books, there is Southey's *Peninsular War*. I am reading that of a morning. You know Southey?' Casaubon's negative response to this question becomes a tacit linking of the old and the introverted:

> 'No,' said Mr. Casaubon, not keeping pace with Mr. Brooke's impetuous reason, and thinking of the book only. 'I have little leisure for such literature just now. I have been using up my eyesight on old characters lately [...] I feed too much on the inward sources; I live too much with the dead. My mind is something like the ghost of an ancient, wandering about the world and trying mentally to construct it as it used to be, in spite of ruin and confusing changes'.[3]

---

3   Eliot, *Middlemorch*, ch. 2.

So far as Southey's celebrated history is concerned, we need look no further than its title page, which quotes as its own epigraph a passage from Polybius: Ἱστορίας γὰρ ἐὰν ἀφέλῃ τις τὸ διὰ τί, καὶ πῶς, καὶ τίνος χάριν ἐπράχθη, καὶ τὸ πραχθὲν πότερα εὔλογον ἔσχε τὸ τέλος, τὸ καταλειπόμενον αὐτῆς ἀγώνισμα μὲν, μάθημα δὲ οὐ γίγνεται· καὶ παραυτίκα μὲν τέρπει, πρὸς δὲ τὸ μέλλον οὐδὲν ὠφελεῖ τὸ παράπαν. This means: 'For if you take from history all explanation of cause, principle, and motive, and of the adaptation of the means to the end, what is left is a mere panorama without being instructive; and, though it may please for the moment, has no abiding value'.[4] Mere panorama is as far as Casaubon ever gets, of course; not because he hasn't had time, or professional expertise, as a collector of data, but because he has missed this fundamental Polybian point.

The question then is not just that Casaubon is mired in the past, but that his comprehension of the past is merely panoramic. Of course, he *is* mired in the past. Indeed, it's possible that Eliot, usually more nuanced in her characterisation, rather over-plays this distinction. In the next chapter Mr. Brooke attempts to interest Casaubon in 'documents on machine-breaking and rick-burning', whilst 'Mr. Casaubon made a dignified though somewhat sad audience; bowed in the right place, and avoided looking at anything documentary as far as possible'. Later in the novel, Ladislaw, famously twitting Casaubon (though not to his face) for his ignorance of German scholarship, lays out the case plainly:

> 'But there are very valuable books about antiquities which were written a long while ago by scholars who knew nothing about these modern things; and they are still used. Why should Mr. Casaubon's not be valuable, like theirs?' said Dorothea, with more remonstrant energy. She was impelled to have the argument aloud, which she had been having in her own mind.
>
> 'That depends on the line of study taken,' said Will, also getting a tone of rejoinder. 'The subject Mr. Casaubon has chosen is as changing as chemistry: new discoveries are constantly making new points of view. Who wants a system on the basis of the four elements, or a book to refute

---

4   Polybius, *Histories*, ed. by Theodorus Büttner-Wobst after L. Dindorf (Leipzig: Teubner, 1893), vol. 3, ch. 31, http://www.perseus.tufts.edu/hopper/text?doc=Pl b.+3.31.&fromdoc=Perseus%3Atext%3A1999.01.0233. The translation is by Eliot's contemporary Evelyn S. Shuckburgh, *The Histories of Polybius* (London: Macmillan & Co., 1889), vol. 1, p. 193.

Paracelsus? Do you not see that it is no use now to be crawling a little way after men of the last century—men like Bryant—and correcting their mistakes?—living in a lumber-room and furbishing up broken-legged theories about Chus and Mizraim?'[5]

With Ladislaw, Eliot draws on a different cultural reservoir to characterise his freshness and youth. For example: in chapter 37, Ladislaw visits Dorothea to tell her he's taking up the editorship of the new Middlemarch newspaper. She is pleased, since it means he will stay in the area, but immediately has second thoughts: it might displease her husband. Accordingly she suggests he obtain Casaubon's blessing:

> 'But my opinion is of little consequence on such a subject. I think you should be guided by Mr. Casaubon. I spoke without thinking of anything else than my own feeling, which has nothing to do with the real question. But it now occurs to me—perhaps Mr. Casaubon might see that the proposal was not wise. Can you not wait now and mention it to him?'

> 'I can't wait to-day,' said Will, inwardly seared by the possibility that Mr. Casaubon would enter. 'The rain is quite over now. I told Mr. Brooke not to call for me: I would rather walk the five miles. I shall strike across Halsell Common, and see the gleams on the wet grass. I like that'.[6]

In the event, of course, Casaubon tries to forbid Ladislaw taking up the position. But, for the moment, what I am interested in is that lovely detail of the wet grass.

Ruskin's five-volume *Modern Painters* (1843–60) is, perhaps, his masterpiece: a sustained interrogation of aesthetics, of the artistic apprehension of nature, and a full-throated defence of the genius of J. M. W. Turner. Eliot read this work, and indeed reviewed it, or at least reviewed volumes three and four.[7] And here is Ruskin praising Turner's 'Salisbury Cathedral':

> The plain is swept by rapid but not distressful rain. The cathedral occupies the centre of the picture, towering high over the city, of which the houses (made on purpose smaller than they really are) are scattered about it like a flock of sheep. The cathedral is surrounded by a great light. The storm gives way at first in a subdued gleam over a distant parish church, then

---

5   Eliot, *Middlemarch*, ch. 22.

6   Ibid., ch. 37.

7   George Eliot, 'Art and Belles Lettres: Review of *Modern Painters*', *Westminster Review*, 65 (April 1856), 625–33.

bursts down again, breaks away into full light. The rain-clouds in this picture are wrought with a care which I have never seen equalled in any other sky of the same kind. It is the rain of blessing—abundant, but full of brightness; golden gleams are flying across the wet grass.[8]

It is possible these Ruskinian details, the rain 'a blessing', the post-storm 'gleams across the wet grass', were in Eliot's mind when she wrote her bit about Ladislaw. It would be a way of reinforcing that he has a painter's eye, a Ruskinian capacity for fine attention to the beauty of nature—which is to say, another way of drawing the contrast with Dorothea's myopic, dryasdust husband. Not that John Ruskin figures as an especially auspicious model when it comes to the case of an older man marrying a younger, idealistic woman, of course. Conceivably that particular irony was also in Eliot's mind.

Eliot touches on the contrast between the future-oriented visual arts, and the library-work of dead textual scholarship, during Dorothea and Casaubon's Roman honeymoon. Dorothea is eager to help her husband's researches:

> In their conversation before marriage, Mr. Casaubon had often dwelt on some explanation or questionable detail of which Dorothea did not see the bearing; but such imperfect coherence seemed due to the brokenness of their intercourse, and, supported by her faith in their future, she had listened with fervid patience to a recitation of possible arguments to be brought against Mr. Casaubon's entirely new view of the Philistine god Dagon and other fish-deities, thinking that hereafter she should see this subject which touched him so nearly from the same high ground whence doubtless it had become so important to him.[9]

We understand that 'Mr. Casaubon's entirely new view of the Philistine god Dagon' is a dead-end. Eliot's novel is not interested in his question. Its concerns are quite other, to do with the relationship between art and life, how love is reconciled to reality and the way life is best lived. Should we wish to dig down a little, we discover that Dagon is a pagan deity mentioned several times in the Bible.[10] The consensus of

---

8   John Ruskin, *Modern Painters*, vol. 5 (London: Smith, Elder & Co., 1860), part 7, ch. 4, section 19, https://www.gutenberg.org/files/44329/44329-h/44329-h.htm

9   Eliot, *Middlemarch*, ch. 22.

10 Judges 16.23 tells how the temple of Dagon is destroyed by Samson at Gaza (Samson's last act, of course: he dies in the ruins he himself makes). Elsewhere we learn that King Saul's severed head was displayed in a different temple of

nineteenth-century scholarship was that he was, as Eliot notes, a pagan fish-god. John McClintock describes him as a kind of merman, 'the body of a fish with the head and hands of a man'.[11]

Horace's *Ars Poetica*, one of the earliest and most influential works of aesthetic theory, opens with these lines:

> *Humano capiti cervicem pictor equinam*
> *iungere si velit, et varias inducere plumas,*
> *undique conlatis membris, ut turpiter atrum*
> *desinat in piscem mulier formosa superne,*
> *spectatum admissi risum teneatis, amici?*[12]

> If a painter should wish to unite a horse's neck to a human head, and spread a variety of plumage over limbs [of different animals] taken from every part of nature, so that what is a beautiful woman in the upper part terminates unsightly in an ugly fish below; could you, my friends, refrain from laughter, were you admitted to such a sight?

Horace takes it for granted that this kind of incongruity is, simply, ludicrous. Art should aim for something better: paint a fish by all means, or paint a beautiful woman, but don't muddle the two up. The *Ars Poetica* is a very famous piece of classical literary criticism, and Eliot certainly knew it: according to John Rignall, Horace is 'the Latin author George Eliot refers to most frequently in her writing'.[13] Was she thinking of the *Ars Poetica*, I wonder, when she prefaces her novel's first sustained discussion of the purpose and form of art with this mermaid-ish reference to Casaubon's pointless researches? Horace's whole

---

Dagon [1 Maccabees 10.83; 11.4] and 1 Samuel 5.2–7 informs us the Ark of the Covenant was seized by the Philistines and taken to Dagon's temple in Ashdod. The Philistines set a fetish of Dagon before their trophy, but each morning they discover it lying prostrate before the ark. They set it upright but the following morning it is discovered fallen over, and on the third morning it is broken into pieces: in the words of KJV, 'the head of Dagon and both the palms of his hands were cut off upon the threshold; only the stump of Dagon was left to him'.

11   John McClintock, *Cyclopaedia of Biblical, Theological, and Ecclesiastical Literature*, 2 vols (New York: Harper, 1868), vol. 2, p. 642.

12   Horace, *De Arte Poetica liber*, ed. by C. Smart (Philadelphia: Joseph Whetham, 1836), 1, http://www.perseus.tufts.edu/hopper/text?doc=Perseus%3Atext%3A1999.02.0 064%3Acard%3D1; Horace, *The Art of Poetry: To the Pisos*, ed. and trans. by C. Smart and Thomas Alois Buckley (New York: Harper and Brothers, 1863), 1, http:// www.perseus.tufts.edu/hopper/text?doc=Perseus%3Atext%3A1999.02.0065%3Ac ard%3D1

13   John Rignall, ed., *Oxford Reader's Companion to George Eliot* (Oxford: Oxford University Press, 2000), p. 166.

point is—to repeat Dorothea's words, quoted above—that appending a scaly fish tail to a human torso is 'a consecration of ugliness rather than beauty' and 'ridiculous'. Eliot tucks the joke in at various places: as with Mrs. Cadwallader's unforgiving judgement that 'Casaubon has money enough; I must do him that justice' but 'as to his blood, I suppose the family quarterings are three cuttle-fish sable, and a commentator rampant'.[14] We laugh because there *is* something 'fishy' about Casaubon. He's a cold fish, in many ways neither fish nor fowl.

Dorothea meets Ladislaw on her honeymoon, in Rome, where Ladislaw is improving his artistic technique by studying under the German artist Adolf Naumann (the Casaubons later visit Naumann's studio and both sit for portraits). Will dines with Mr. and Mrs. Casaubon and the conversation turns to art, a topic over which he and Dorothea disagree. 'I fear you are a heretic about art generally', Ladislaw tells her and she replies that the important thing would be to make life itself beautiful, rather than make beautiful imitations of life:

> I should like to make life beautiful—I mean everybody's life. And then all this immense expense of art, that seems somehow to lie outside life and make it no better for the world, pains one. It spoils my enjoyment of anything when I am made to think that most people are shut out from it. [...] I should be quite willing to enjoy the art here [in Rome], but there is so much that I don't know the reason of—so much that seems to me a consecration of ugliness rather than beauty. The painting and sculpture may be wonderful, but the feeling is often low and brutal, and sometimes even ridiculous.[15]

Dorothea adds 'I have often felt since I have been in Rome that most of our lives would look much uglier and more bungling than the pictures, if they could be put on the wall'. It is an important aesthetic question: should art be 'realist', and serve the betterment of life, or 'idealist' adding a beautifying and ennobling sheen to the things represented? But this is not a question that engages Casaubon, devoted as he is to his myopic pedantry. When Ladislaw praises the ambition of Neumann's art ('"The sketch must be very grand, if it conveys so much," said Dorothea. "Oh yes," said Will, laughing, "and migrations of races and clearings of forests—and America and the steam-engine. Everything you can

---

14   Eliot, *Middlemarch*, ch. 6.
15   Ibid., ch. 22.

imagine!"') Dorothea suggests, 'smiling towards her husband' that it would require somebody of Casaubon's encyclopaedic knowledge 'to be able to read it'. Eliot adds: 'Mr. Casaubon blinked furtively at Will. He had a suspicion that he was being laughed at. But it was not possible to include Dorothea in the suspicion'.

What, then, of Casaubon's 'entirely new view of the Philistine god Dagon'? Eliot, of course, is writing about 'real' people in 'real' situations, and not about horseheaded men and fishtailed women of fantasy or (latterly) science fiction. Where Eliot's 'literary realism' embodies a mimetic logic, whereby life is mapped onto art with a minimum of distortion, science fiction and fantasy are both metaphorical modes of art, because they aim to represent the world without reproducing it. The metaphors that inform science fiction sometimes calcify, through over-use, into mere cliché: the robot, the spaceship, the raygun. But at its best, science fiction estranges its reader with an eloquent and arresting metaphorical apprehension of life that compels us again to think about existence. Speaking for myself, and as a writer of science fiction, I *value* that estrangement, and consider metaphor a more expressive mode of art than mimesis. And under that aegis, Casaubon's merman seems to me a fascinating rebus for a novel like *Middlemarch*—a novel, after all, centrally about the way human life and its relationships so often construe incompatible juxtapositions: Dorothea and Casaubon, Lydgate and Rosamond, high ideals and provincial practicalities. These are the petty hypocrisies of the respectable middle classes that Matthew Arnold so memorably called 'philistinism'.

In the Old Testament Dagon appears as the enemy of righteousness, but by the time we get to the New Testament we must consider a new dispensation, one in which the last now becomes the first. After all, what is Christ himself if not a kind of fish god? He recruits disciples from trawlermen telling them to become fishers of men; he feeds five thousand, miraculously, with 'five small loaves and two fish'. In another miracle he tells Peter that he will be able to pay the temple tax by casting a line in the water, saying that a coin will be found in the fish's mouth, which it is. In Matthew 12:38–45 Jesus identifies himself with 'the Sign of Jonah', symbolic of his death and resurrection. The early church branded itself with a fish symbol (many modern Christians do the same): ICHTHUS, which means fish, and is a Greek acrostic (IXΘΥΣ).

Conceivably Casaubon's key to all mythologies would, if completed, prove to be a way of reconciling pagan and Christian piscine symbols into one unified whole.

I daresay that strikes you as fanciful. But this question of 'Realism' versus the Fantastic had important resonances for Eliot's own religious faith. In 1846 she had translated David Strauss's *Das Leben Jesu*, in its day a controversial book (the Earl of Shaftesbury memorably called Eliot's translation 'the most pestilential book ever vomited out of the jaws of hell'). Strauss conceded that Christ was a historical figure but argued that there had been nothing supernatural or miraculous about his ministry. The miracles recorded in the New Testament were, he suggested, mythic accretions or fanciful extrapolations added-in by the early Church bolster their messiah's reputation as a wonder-worker. Eliot was persuaded by this argument. Then again, it is possible to disbelieve the miraculous events recorded in the Bible without altogether jettisoning one's engagement with the orientations of faith. In the words of Sean Gaston: 'Eliot rejected the supernatural trappings of punishment and reward, while still embracing what is in "conformity with the will of the Supreme" [...] though she later modified her youthful vehemence against orthodoxy, by and large her position appears to have remained unchanged for the rest of her life'.[16] Christianity can be a rationalist faith, and a believer can think of Christ as a character in, as it were, a realist story. Then again, Christianity can be a miraculous faith, and a believer can think of Christ as a practitioner of the strongest kind of magic. Calling Christ a kind of fish-god is to take the latter line (the fish stories in the New Testament all share a miraculous element). Seem this way, Christianity itself becomes is a kind of numinous monster, a combination of the ordinary and the impossible, the mundane and the magical. A kind of merman or mermaid system of belief. Monsters can, as Horace says, be ridiculous, or ugly, but they can also be marvellous. It is even possible that some monsters can be marvellous *because* they are ridiculous and ugly. Metaphor itself is a yoking together of apparent incompatibles in the service of a new eloquence.

The truth is, critics have never quite decided on the place of Casaubon's 'Key to All Mythologies' in *Middlemarch*. In one sense, of

---

16 Sean Gaston, 'George Eliot and the Anglican Reader', *Literature and Theology*, 31.3 (2017), 318–37 (p. 319), https://doi.org/10.1093/litthe/frw026

course, it is obvious enough: this unfinished and perhaps unfinishable project is indicative of Casaubon's unfittedness as Dorothea's husband. She deserves better than this withered old pedant, wholly consumed by his dryasdust obsessions. From the novel's first mention of the character, his project is linked to his name, as something integral to his being-in-the-world: 'the Reverend Edward Casaubon, noted in the county as a man of profound learning, understood for many years to be engaged on a great work concerning religious history'.[17] The very phrase 'Key to All Mythologies' has become a shorthand for pointless and pedantic scholarly vanity, the academic's 'life project' always doomed to failure—as an academic myself, I can vouch for how sharply the jibe can hit home.

The fact Dorothea is initially won-over by Casaubon's plan speaks to the naivety of her character at the novel's beginning; and her slowly dawning realisation of the barrenness of her husband's work tracks her own Bildungsroman narrative—that is, her growth and development. So, in that sense, it's obvious enough what function the 'Key' has in the novel.

But here's what I'm not sure about: is the problem with Casaubon's 'Key' that it is too ambitiously framed, doomed by virtue of the fact that it seeks to explain everything with one *clef* when the nature of reality—the reality Eliot so deftly gestures towards with her particular mode of literary realism—is too complex to admit of such simplistic analysis? Or is the idea that a 'Key' could be written so as to explain all mythological systems but that Casaubon is too disorganised, too narrow-minded and too lacking in necessary expertise, to do it? (Later in the story Ladislaw scoffs that Casaubon doesn't even read German.) Is the novel saying that the 'Key to All Mythologies' could never be written, or is it saying that such a work *could* be written, just not by Casaubon?

Casaubon believes his 'Key' will show 'that all the mythical systems or erratic mythical fragments in the world were corruptions of a tradition originally revealed'[18] and though he has a relatively high opinion of Dorothea's intelligence compared to other women, he does not propose to take her on as a partner. Her role is to be 'helpmeet', 'secretary', to take dictation and assist him in sorting through paperwork. In chapter 2 we learn that the materials for the 'Key' are dispersed between many

---

17   Eliot, *Middlemarch*, ch. 1.
18   Ibid., ch. 3.

pigeon-holes in Casaubon's study, and Dorothea believes she could be the person to order and arrange the material. When Mr. Brooke complains that *his* pigeonholes are a mess ('I have tried pigeon-holes, but everything gets mixed in pigeon-holes: I never know whether a paper is in A or Z') Dorothea's offer to him—'I wish you would let me sort your papers for you, uncle. I would letter them all, and then make a list of subjects under each letter'—is actually a coded romantic pitch at Casaubon, and is, in the cleverly-observed, rather strangulated idiom in which Eliot renders this doomed love affair, recognised as such ('Mr. Casaubon gravely smiled approval').

We could rephrase my question this way: is Dorothea culpably naïve for believing in Casaubon's proposed 'Key'? I'm not sure she is. Casaubon's work is, on its face, a perfectly respectable project. As Colin Kidd's recent study, *The World of Mr Casaubon*, shows, there was a rich tradition of comparative mythology through the eighteenth- and nineteenth-centuries—a 'significant and variegated terrain' rather than the 'sterile, unworldly disengagement of which Mr. Casaubon has for so long been an emblem'.[19] Despite taking its name from Eliot's famous scholar, Kidd's book is not really about *Middlemarch*. Its three sections examine, first, 'the eighteenth-century golden age' of such research, second 'the Age of Revolution and Reform down to the early 1830s, the period in which the novel is immediately set' when 'mythography remained an urgent calling for Anglican scholars who wished to conserve Christian truth against the poisons of Enlightenment deism, scepticism and atheism', and finally the period from the 1830s to the novel's publication 1870–71, the time 'during which Eliot's own views of mythography were formed'.[20] Lots of people were researching and writing 'Keys'. There was, Kidd implies, nothing hubristic or outrageous about Casaubon attempting such a thing.

Perhaps our mistake is focusing on the 'Key' part of Casaubon's title. Compare the real-world Ernest von Bunsen, eminent scholar of comparative religion and mythology, who published his *Key of Knowledge* (in English) in 1865. His 'Key' is: Christ (Bunsen, an eminent Anglo-German writer and contemporary of Eliot's, proposed a common origin

---

19 Colin Kidd, *The World of Mr Casaubon: Britain's Wars of Mythography, 1700–1870* (Cambridge: Cambridge University Press, 2016), p. 2, https://doi.org/10.1017/9781139226646

20 Ibid., p. 7.

for many different religions and mythologies, including Buddhism, Essene Judaism and paganism: his book's full title is *The Hidden Wisdom of Christ and the Key of Knowledge*). Were it ever finished, Casaubon's book would—presumably—argue similarly that all the various mythological traditions derive, with varying degrees of corruption and divergence, from the sacred revelation of the Christian God. When the German painter Naumann sees Casaubon and Dorothea on their honeymoon together in Rome he assumes the man is a Geistlicher, a clergyman or cleric.

Nor was such a theory eccentric by the standards of the age. Casaubon's theory has the same shape, and therefore the same structurally explanatory power, as the theory proposed by the era's most famous comparative mythographer, Max Müller, who argued that myth and language could be traced back to a common linguistic and cultural origin-point he named 'Aryan' (now generally called 'Indo-European'). So, for example: Müller traces the word for 'god' back through history (*dieu, deus, theos* and so on) to a now lost Proto-Indo-European word **dyiw* that means 'sky, heavens, sun'. You can identify that with your personal God, or make an observation about humankind's propensity to religiosity more generally, but either way it is a perfectly Casaubonic argument. And we know that Eliot read Müller closely.

Eliot's critics, incidentally, have not been shy when it comes to picking up Casaubon's dropped baton, offering a whole ring of keys of their own to the *Middlemarch* myth. According to Paul Milton 'inheritance law' is not just one of the novel's various interests, it is the Casaubonic key to everything.[21] For Lisa Baltazar, Casaubon's project exists in the novel so that Eliot can undertake 'an extremely informed debunking' of infallibilist Biblical criticism.[22] And for Roger Travis the 'Key' turns out to be Dorothea herself. Travis argues that Dorothea resists the 'mummification' implicit in husband's struggle with Truth by stepping out of the textual 'labyrinth' into life itself: '*Middlemarch* is a labyrinth like the social life of Middlemarch like the *Key*', he argues, 'and Dorothea's

---

21   Paul Milton, 'Inheritance as the Key to all Mythologies: George Eliot and Legal Practice', *Mosaic: A Journal for the Interdisciplinary Study of Literature*, 28.1 (1995), 49–68.

22   Lisa Baltazar, 'The Critique of Anglican Biblical Scholarship in George Eliot's *Middlemarch*', *Literature and Theology*, 15.1 (2001), 40–60 (p. 40), https://doi.org/10.1093/litthe/15.1.40

winding path through them makes emphatically satisfying her final achievement of a purity and legibility'. The Key, then, is 'Dorothea's character': 'with her, the reader must lay aside notions of a mythology that lacks animate life, an epic that fossilizes' and instead learn 'the art of living'.[23]

In other words, perhaps the problem with a 'Key to all Mythologies' isn't the *key* part, so much as the *mythologies* part. Myths fascinated Eliot, as they do most of us. They are, after all, powerful and enduring stories, pitched somewhere between fiction and faith. And it goes without saying that stories are central to a novelist's praxis. Generations of readers can confirm Eliot's skill at telling them. At the same time, Eliot is fascinated by the idea that some stories *can't* be told using the conventional or traditional forms and structures. In one sense the whole of *Middlemarch* tends to the point where Eliot says to her readers: 'now Dorothea passes out of view of the kinds of stories that constitute novels like mine'. Earlier in the book she is compared, or compares herself, to figures from both religious and classical myth—Saint Theresa and Antigone amongst various others—but by the end her life is revealed to be just her life, not shaped or directed by any such template. This in turn might suggest another perspective on Casaubon's notorious 'Key': not that it is too ambitious to be achieved but on the contrary that it is, perhaps, *too facile*—that it is only too easy to extract some guiding principle from 'mythology' and apply it to our lives, where the truth is that to live properly means not confusing such models with actuality. Life—as George Eliot tells us, paradoxically enough, using her story—*is not a story*.

Casaubon's problem is not that he is seeking an impossible key. He already possesses the key. His problem is that he thinks this key fits the lock marked 'mythologies' when (Eliot is saying) it actually fits the lock marked 'life'. *Middlemarch* ends not because there's nothing more for Dorothea to do, but on the contrary because she has a whole life to live, and because life is bent out of the true when writers try to fit it into those procrustean structures called 'stories', from myths to novels. Look again at the novel's desperately famous last lines. 'The effect of

---

23   Roger Travis, 'From "Shattered Mummies" to "An Epic Life": Casaubon's Key to All Mythologies and Dorothea's Mythic Renewal in George Eliot's *Middlemarch*', *International Journal of the Classical Tradition*, 5.3 (1999), 367–82 (pp. 380–81), https://doi.org/10.1007/bf02687693

her being on those around her was incalculably diffusive' is surely a direct nod—'Diffusionism' is the name given to the theories of Müller and his ilk, that myth, religion and culture spread and diffuse from one source across the world. Here Eliot revisits the governing principle of Casaubon's 'Key' in order to relocate it from myth to life—where, she seems to be saying, it belongs, for life should be lived not only unobtrusively but faithfully. But now I am straying into the matter of the final chapter: the ending of this novel, and its beginning. The way epigraphs concertina their beginning and their end (nobody wants an epigraph that goes on for pages and pages; the pithier the better) and the way they parse this spacious novel, a work whose beginning and end are separated by hundreds of thousands of words, and yet are closely interconnected.

Ladislaw, though, believes in art insofar as it addresses and offers amelioration to the age in which he actually lives. He is a realist, we might say, in art as in politics; although the debate he has with Lydgate over dinner in chapter forty-six sees him dismissed as a dreamer: 'crying up a [political] measure as if it were a universal cure [...] encouraging the superstitious exaggeration of hopes about this particular measure'. To Lydgate all party politics is 'a political hocus-pocus'. Ladislaw, however, considers himself a pragmatist: 'my dear fellow, but your cure must begin somewhere, and put it that a thousand things which debase a population can never be reformed without this particular reform to begin with'.[24] The novel in which he appears is a more hybrid entity: and one of the functions of many of its embedded quotations and epigraphs is to construe the novel as simultaneously (what we might call) 'realism' and something that expresses a mythic, even a monstrous truth in the way human lives are shaped and lived. And this brings me to the matter of Eliot's allusiveness to classical legend and literature.

---

24   Eliot, *Middlemarch*, ch. 46.

6. Myth, *Middlemarch* and the *Mill*

Out in Mid-Sea

The epigraph to chapter 44 reads as follows:

> I would not creep along the coast, but steer
> Out in mid-sea, by guidance of the stars.

This little couplet is about Dorothea leaving behind the shore-hugging life she has had with Casaubon and charting a more adventurous and exciting (sexual) course. Or at least it is about her starting to think, obliquely, in these terms. In chapter 44, Casaubon is dying but not dead, and Dorothea, walking around the hospital grounds, is thinking about her future.

Critics assume these two lines were written by Eliot herself, which is partly correct. In fact, 'creep along the coast' is a phrase from John Dryden's *The Hind and the Panther* (1687), and the six-line passage in which it occurs rather looks like it has been boiled down by Eliot for her two.

> Why choose we, then, like Bilanders, to creep
> Along the coast, and land in view to keep,
> When safely we may launch into the deep?
> In the same vessel which our Saviour bore,
> Himself the pilot, let us leave the shore,
> And with a better guide a better world explore.[1]

(A 'bilander' is a flat-bottomed masted Dutch ship, designed for coastal traffic.) This piously Christian sentiment is, at root, classical. The contrast

---

[1] John Dryden, *The Hind and the Panther: A Poem, in Three Parts* (London: Printed for Jacob Tonson, 1687), part 1, ll. 128–33, http://www.online-literature.com/dryden/poetical-works-vol1/15/

     https://doi.org/10.11647/OBP.0249.06

between hugging the shore and the more dangerous but far-reaching tactic of heading out across open water defined classical navigation. The Greeks even had a particular name for the former activity. Here's Nicholas Purcell in the *Oxford Classical Dictionary*:

> *Periploi*, 'voyages around' (i.e. around a sea, following the coastline), were the standard basis of ancient descriptive geography. Sequences of harbours, landings, watering-places, shelters from bad weather, landmarks, or hazards could be remembered in an oral tradition as a sometimes very long list, and in written culture provided a summation of space that could be easier to intuit, and which offered much more room for detail, than cartography.[2]

More adventurous Greek heroes repudiate such timid periplism. Here's Homer's *Odyssey*:

> Gladly then did goodly Odysseus spread his sail to the breeze; and he sat and guided his raft skilfully with the steering-oar, nor did sleep fall upon his eyelids, as he watched the Pleiads, and late-setting Bootes, and the Bear, which men also call the Wain, which ever circles where it is and watches Orion, and alone has no part in the baths of Ocean. For this star Calypso, the beautiful goddess, had bidden him to keep on the left hand as he sailed over the sea. For seventeen days then he sailed over the sea, and on the eighteenth appeared the shadowy mountains of the land of the Phaeacians, where it lay nearest to him; and it shewed like unto a shield in the misty deep.[3]

Might Eliot have had this Homeric moment in mind in writing her couplet she sets as the epigraph to chapter 44? One of the (if you'll excuse me) oddities of the *Odyssey* is that its overarching storyline—a man travelling back through adversity to reunite with his beloved wife—is interrupted by stories of that same man pairing-off with women *not* his wife, and finding himself repeatedly tangled-up in the narratological logic of sexual romance. Item: Odysseus loiters with Circe. Item: he flirts with Nausicaa. Item: as the epic opens he is cohabiting with the beautiful nymph Calypso. Indeed, it is leaving Calypso's island that occasions the

---

2   Nicholas Purcell, '*Periploi*: Voyages around', *Oxford Classical Dictionary* (2015), https://oxfordre.com/classics/view/10.1093/acrefore/9780199381135.001.0001/acrefore-9780199381135-e-4872

3   Homer, *Odyssey*, trans. by A. T. Murray (London: William Heinemann, 1919), book 5, ll. 270–82, https://www.perseus.tufts.edu/hopper/text?doc=Perseus%3Atext%3A1999.01.0136%3Abook%3D5%3Acard%3D262

passage quoted above, where Odysseus sets out, not creeping along the shore, but steering out in mid-sea by guidance of the stars.

And where is he heading? To the land of the Phaeacians, where he meets the beautiful young Phaeacian princess Nausicaa and afterwards captivates her with stories of his many adventures. It reads as the set-up to a romantic story that ought to end with Odysseus marrying Nausicaa, although (of course) it doesn't. Instead of that romantic ending, the story makes a knight's-move into a different denouement: the Phaeacians gift Odysseus quantities of treasure and send him on his way back to his actual wife.

One could not call Odysseus sexually faithful, certainly. There's always seemed to me something ironic in the poem's happy ending, predicated as it is upon his supposedly happy reunion with Penelope, who has gone to such extraordinary lengths to *avoid* cheating on her husband. And as *Middlemarch* moves into its second half it reveals itself as, amongst other things, a meditation on the nature of marital infidelity, not (of course) as actual physical adultery, but as a complication of the wedded heart. Casaubon, fretful at the prospect of Dorothea having sex with Ladislaw, decides that such a connection would constitute adultery even after his death; and so he arranges his posthumous testament to try and prevent it. We, as readers, naturally don't see it that way—a widow should surely be allowed to marry again without acquiring the taint of adultery. And Dorothea is hardly Odysseus, jumping into bed with whomever she comes across. And yet she *is* conflicted. The story wouldn't be half so interesting if she weren't. Which is to say: it's not about the money that she would lose if she marries Ladislaw, or not only about that. There's something else at work in her sexual conscience.

We flatten the dramatic dilemma of the novel's second half if we take an absolutist moral position with respect to it: as it might be, telling ourselves *Casaubon is wholly irrational in demanding his widow be sexually chaste after his death; Dorothea is wholly within her rights to take another husband and should feel no scruple about desiring another man*. It's a fair enough position, but it runs the risk of missing what Eliot is doing. She is not an absolutist writer—always fonder, we might say, as per her title, of the middle line. Say Dorothea has been guilty, even self-deceiving, about her desire for Ladislaw whilst her husband was alive. Those are the kinds of feelings (the guilt, I mean) that don't merely evaporate now that her husband is dead. In other words, I'm suggesting Eliot is saying there is something *complicated* in our married lives: something adulterated about our desire for our spouses even in the most untroubled of marriages (and you wouldn't call Casaubon and Dorothea's marriage untroubled). Odysseus and Penelope, we might say, are closer to the truth of marriage than Sir Charles Grandison and Lady Harriet. If that weren't the case, the psychodrama of *Middlemarch* would be considerably less compelling than it actually is.

Rosamond has no such Dorothean scruples. Indeed, immediately before this chapter (and its *Odyssean* epigraph) she, newly married to Lydgate, finds herself awaking into a worldly awareness of the potency of, precisely, extra-marital sexual allure:

> Rosamond felt herself beginning to know a great deal of the world, especially in discovering what when she was in her unmarried girlhood had been inconceivable to her except as a dim tragedy in by-gone costumes—that women, even after marriage, might make conquests and enslave men. At that time young ladies in the country, even when educated at Mrs. Lemon's, read little French literature later than Racine, and public prints had not cast their present magnificent illumination over the scandals of life. Still, vanity, with a woman's whole mind and day to work in, can construct abundantly on slight hints, especially on such a hint as the possibility of indefinite conquests. How delightful to make captives from the throne of marriage with a husband as crown-prince by your side—himself in fact a subject—while the captives look up forever hopeless, losing their rest probably, and if their appetite too, so much the better![4]

'What can a man do when he takes to adoring one of you mermaids?' her poor husband wonders, aloud, unconsciously anticipating the nautical metaphor. What indeed? There are a great many Victorian novels about the scandal of bigamous marriage, not because bigamy was a particular problem in the nineteenth-century, but because this was one of the ways authors could navigate the conventions of nineteenth-century respectability and representation so as to talk about a more basic, universal human fact: that lines of desire do not always align themselves with the marriage bond.

It is worth saying a little more about the Homer to which Eliot alludes here. It had become well-known by the 1870s that Homer's

---

4   Eliot, *Middlemarch*, ch. 43.

epics were stitched together from a variety of earlier myths and stories (although it wasn't until the twentieth century that the full scope of the oral deep-history of 'Homer'—and his likely non-existence— was finally established). In the case of the episode with Nausicaa what has happened, evidently, is that Homer has integrated into his epic an older 'romance' story, in which the beautiful princess helps the shipwrecked stranger who turns out to be a great prince who in turn wins her heart with his magnificent storytelling. Everything in this portion of the *Odyssey* points us in this direction—except that it doesn't work out that way. Except that this isn't the direction the story goes down (it can't, because Odysseus already has a wife). Something about this implied but broken-off romantic emplotment interests me, and interests me especially with respect to *Middlemarch*. I am certainly not the only reader who sees, in Eliot's twinned stories of Dorothea and Lydgate—originally planned as two separate novels, of course— an as-it-were Nausicaa/Odysseus implicit-tale of thwarted possibility, in many ways the perfect couple: both young, beautiful, idealistic, driven. Of course they can't be together because Dorothea is married, and by the time she is free to marry again Lydgate is married. And I concede there's nothing in the novel that explicitly reverts to any mutual attraction between them.

Indeed, my point is less about the *will-they-won't-they?* clichés of love story narrative (in this case more of a *might-they-could-they-have?*). Rather, it is about the balance of mode: just as the *Odyssey* contains laminations of romance and folk-tale in its broader matrix of 'epic', *Middlemarch* accommodates pockets of melodrama, as with Lydgate's backstory with Mme Laure, or Dorothea's falling into blank verse, within its defining logic of scientific—I am arguing, medical and microscopic—realism.

It raises questions of how capacious the novel may be in terms of accommodating other modes. Maybe there are some things fundamentally immiscible with the form of the novel. It is a question particularly worth raising with respect to Eliot, since she was not only unusually well-read for a major Victorian novelist in the Classics, but she also had specific aesthetic interests in trying to recreate aspects of classical form in contemporary novelistic textual production. Most famously, she attempted in *The Mill on the Floss* (1860) to clothe in the lineaments of modern fiction the gravity, the shape and the affect of Attic tragedy. If *Mill* is Eliot essaying tragedy, could we describe *Middlemarch* as an attempt to head out, mid-sea, into classical epic?

The counter-argument is easy enough to frame. 'Prose romance' stretches back to the Ancient Greeks, but 'the novel' is a basically an eighteenth- and nineteenth-century development, and although it has now spread globally it still manifests a particular, European, bourgeois-Protestant logic. Ian Watt's *Rise of the Novel* is half a century old now, and while there are good reasons to be dissatisfied with it (particularly its near total neglect of female writers) its core thesis still has contemporary critical currency: namely, that 'the distinctive literary qualities of the novel' relate directly to 'those of the society in which it began and flourished', and that it's a form that rises in step with changes in the reading public, of the rise of economic individualism, and of the 'spread of Protestantism, especially in its Calvinist or Puritan forms'.[5] The novel as a mode starts, in other words, as a bourgeois mode of art pitched to a readership largely drawn from the rising middle-class, focusing on things that mattered to them and reflecting their values back upon them. So: individualied, self-reliant characters. So: detailed descriptions of material possessions (houses, furniture, clothes etc), and a particular emphasis on courtship narratives framed in terms of prosperity. So also: the mode's hospitality to Bildungsroman, a spiritualisation of economic growth and return on investments.

If Watt's thesis is correct then we might expect the novel, formally speaking, to work for some things better than others; and we might even argue that there are some things that the novel is just really poor at capturing. And rather than continuing to talk in windy generalisations I might ask a specific question, one with particular relevance to Eliot's art: *can the novel do tragedy?*

It is clearly, of course, possible to write a novel in which characters suffer and die, and even to reproduce, should an author be so minded, the lineaments of a Sophoclean or Shakespearian play in prose. But does tragedy, as tragedy, *work* in the novel? This seems to me at once a question about the specific form of the novel and a question about our larger cultural addiction to happy endings and disinclination to follow the pity and the terror to its logical catharsis-end. Disney's *The Lion King*

5   Ian Watt, *The Rise of the Novel: Studies in Defoe, Richardson and Fielding* (Berkeley: University of California Press, 1957), pp. 7, 60.

is *Hamlet*, yes; but it's Hamlet-With-A-Happy-Ending, which is in a very large sense to miss the point of *Hamlet*. Terry Eagleton agrees with Henri Peyre that the novel as a mode simply isn't hospitable to tragedy:

> A tragic theatre bound up with the despotic absolutism, courtly intrigue, traditional feuds, rigid laws of kinship, codes of honour, cosmic-world-views and faith in destiny gives way to the more rational, hopeful, realist, pragmatic ideologies of the middle class. What rules now is less fate than human agency [...] The public realm of tragedy, with its high-pitched rhetoric and fateful economy, is abandoned for the privately consumed, more expansive, ironic, everyday language of prose fiction. And this [...] is certainly a loss: some critics, as Henri Peyre suggests, blame the death of tragedy on the novel, which 'captured the essentials of tragic emotion, while diluting and often cheapening it'.[6]

Eagleton thinks that tragedy qua tragedy depends upon precisely that public, focused, elevated authenticity that has been dissolved away by the privately consumed art of the novel, novels being more expansive, ironic, told in everyday language and concerning ordinary people.

To test his claim we might look at a specific case study, although it is part of Eagleton's argument that proper examples are thin on the ground. Samuel Richardson's *Pamela* is a twisted sort of courtship novel and comic in generic terms, and although his next novel *Clarissa* spins a similar story into not marriage but the heroine's death, it is difficult to make the case that it generates properly tragic momentum. Leo Tolstoy's *Anna Karenina* lacks the tragic focus of, say, the *Antigone*, not just because Tolstoy is committed to balancing Anna's downward path with his account of Levin's upward one, but because its one main purpose is to create a widescreen portrait of a whole society, which necessarily diffuses the tragic focus we find in Sophocles. Eliot's *The Mill on the Floss* provides a clearer example, if only because in it Eliot undertook a deliberate exercise in re-writing Greek tragedy as a contemporary English novel, and because Eliot is a great writer.

To be more specific, Eliot, the admirer of Sophocles, undertook several approaches by way of transferring, from Greek into English, from drama into this new mode of fiction, a quasi-Sophoclean heft and expressiveness. Above all she loved the *Antigone*, and we can intuit

---

6   Terry Eagleton, *Sweet Violence: The Idea of the Tragic* (Oxford: Blackwell Publishers, 2003), p. 178.

reasons for that in her private life: openly living with the already-married George Henry Lewes put her beyond the pale of many in polite Victorian society, and her own brother Issac, with whom she had been extremely close as a child, cut off all communication with her. After decades of happiness together, Lewes died in 1878. A couple of years later, in 1880, Eliot married a young admirer called John Cross. Only then, with priggish self-satisfaction, did her brother re-open communications with his sister.

So, yes: we can see why Sophocles' great play, with its potent swirl of pseudo-erotic connection between sister and brother superseding the conventions of society at large (even unto death) and its portrait of a wilful individual woman following her heart rather than surrendering to the pressures of convention, spoke so directly to Eliot. She often wrote about it. In her 'The *Antigone* and its Moral', she defined the central problem in Sophocles' play as lying between 'reverence for the gods' and 'the duties of citizenship: two principles, both having their validity, are at war with each'; the conflict between 'the strength of man's intellect, or moral sense, or affection' and 'the rules which society has sanctioned'. Her essay draws a general conclusion: 'whenever man's moral vision collides with social convention the opposition between Antigone and Creon is renewed'.[7]

There is much we could say about Eliot's preference for Sophocles over Aeschylus and Euripides, but there is one thing that's peculiarly relevant to Eliot's project as a novelist I think, and it goes back to Sophocles' great innovation in the drama itself. Aeschylus, we're told, was the first writer to introduce a second actor on stage (before him dramas consisted of a single actor interacting with the chorus). But Sophocles is the first dramatist to introduce a *third* actor and suddenly, we might say, things start to get interesting. George Eliot, certainly, was fascinated by the dramatic, ethical and expressive possibilities of this triangulation, and it is the fundamental interpersonal structure of *The Mill on the Floss*: Maggie Tulliver, her older brother Tom and their father; Maggie, Tom and little Lucy (whom, in a fit of childish jealousy, Maggie pushes in the mud); Maggie, Tom and sensitive, hunchback Philip Wakem, at least until their father's ruination at the hands (as Tom sees it) of Philip's lawyer father makes him put an end to Maggie and

---

7   George Eliot, 'The Antigone and its Moral', *Leader*, 7 (March 29, 1856), 306.

Philip's burgeoning relationship. Then, as the novel moves into its final straight, the story focuses on Maggie, cousin Lucy and Lucy's fiancé Stephen Guest, a more conventional love-triangle.

This final situation brings to the fore the main (as it were) triangulation of the novel: one, Maggie; two, the object of her love—the sexual connection she has with Stephen, the spiritual and intellectual connection she has with Philip—and three, her larger familial and social context;, powerful represented by the blood connection she has with Tom. The main theme of the novel, of course, is that Maggie comes into conflict with larger, impersonal but restrictive forces, of economic necessity, gender oppression and, when she runs away with Stephen, of moral disapprobation. This latter is most forcefully manifested in Tom's individual disapproval, just as the worst aspect of Eliot's (patchy, in truth) social ostracism was the way her beloved brother Isaac cut her:

> At the centre of *The Mill on the Floss* lies the human dilemma from Sophocles' *Antigone* that George Eliot believed to be permanent: the conflict between the conventions of society and individual judgment. An honourable but conventional person, Tom Tulliver, clashes with his more imaginative sister Maggie over these opposing claims [...] Tom seeks conventional honour in exacting middle-class conventionalism; but Maggie seeks honor in her ideals of love and charity. In many ways Tom symbolises the Old Law, Maggie the New.[8]

Eliot also works structurally, as it were: setting out in this novel formally to reproduce the structure of a Greek drama. What I mean by this that Attic tragedy follows a particular formal pattern. In any given Greek tragedy there's an opening speech by a character or a god, that sets the scene: this is called the *parodos*. The bulk of the play consists of *stasima* (a *stasimon* is a choral ode) alternating with episodes (*epei(s)-odia*, 'between the odes') in which two, or later three, actors interact with each other and with the chorus. Things end with an *exodos*. How many episodes should there be? In Greek drama there could be as few as three, or as many as six. In Seneca and Roman tragedy, which largely adopted its formal conventions from the Greek, the number of episodes was mostly five, which is where Renaissance theatre derives its convention that a play should have five acts. Eliot, however, is very particularly not copying

---

8   David Moldstad, '*The Mill on the Floss* and *Antigone*', *PMLA*, 85.3 (1970), 527–31 (p.527), https://doi.org/10.2307/1261454

Shakespeare or even Seneca in her tragic novel, but instead going back to the Sophoclean source. What this means is that *Floss* has a *parodos* in its first chapter, whose narrator ('I remember those large dipping willows, I remember the stone bridge...') takes on the role of chorus. The episodes of the story are interspersed with stasimon-like commentary by the narrator and number, I would argue, six: [1] Maggie's youth; [2] the family's loss of the Mill; [3] Maggie's friendship with Philip; [4] Tom's recovery of the fortune, Tulliver horsewhipping Wakem and dying of an apoplexy; [5] Maggie's affair with Stephen; [6] the Flood. In each case Eliot interposes narrative with observation, commentary and sections of what amount, almost, to prose poetry in describing the world she has created. The *exodos* is Eliot's 'Conclusion'.

The Greek element exists beneath the surface, as it were, of a thoroughly and minutely realised English idiom—the same idiom that Eliot would refine and hone, without such specific Classical underpinning, ten years later for *Middlemarch*. In this earlier novel Eliot does sophisticated things with the Greek mode of externalising interior states and the novelistic mode of internalising them. So, for example: Philip Wakem is *physically* deformed, but Mr. Tulliver is *emotionally* or *psychologically* deformed, a fact reflected in his surname, since the Greek τυλιος, *tulios*, from τυλη, means 'lumpy or hunchbacked'. Eliot plays many such Greek games in her novel: whilst 'St Oggs' is a perfectly English sounding name, perhaps related (we might think) to the Gaelic 'Ogham' we can also note that the Greek ὄγκος, *ogkos*, means 'pride, self-importance, pretension', as well as 'swelling, tumour'. 'The Floss' is another very English sounding name, from the Old-English for 'flow' [cf. the German *flosz*, river]. But then we turn to the Greek verb φλύω to find that it means 'to boil over, to bubble up, to overrun', but also 'to babble, to fill up with words', both of which are peculiarly appropriate to this work.

That said, not every critic has seen Maggie as a straightforward Antigone.

> Clearly Maggie shares Antigone's strong-minded rebellious spirit, and her 'sisterly piety', and she too is torn by opposing principles 'at war with each other.' But when we consider Maggie's case she seems to be divided by principles of a very different kind to those exerting their contrary influence on Antigone. Opposing Maggie's version of 'sisterly

piety' and 'reverence for the gods' [...] are not the 'duties of citizenship' as for Antigone, but rather other forms of feeling, or in Eliot's vocabulary, varieties of sympathy: her compassion for Philip Wakem and her passion for Stephen Guest.[9]

'Maggie's dilemma', argues McDonagh, in a point to which I'll return in a moment, 'seems reducible to a conflict not of laws or duties but of *feelings*, and indeed feelings for opposing men; the father and brother versus the friend and the lover'. It is interesting, and may or may not be significant, that *Mill on the Floss* contains no explicit references at all to the *Antigone*. Maybe Eliot felt she didn't need to spell out explicitly what was so obvious; but that doesn't seem to have been her practice elsewhere. Take Philip Wakem, the intelligent, sensitive crippled boy whom Maggie rejects (because he's ugly, and then because her brother tells her to) but whose quiet, empathetic intellect proves essential to Maggie's own spiritual growth. It seems clear to me that he is called Philip in allusion to Sophocles' magic cripple Philoctetes; and it seems that way in part because Eliot all but lays it out. When they are still children, Tom injures his foot, and during his convalescence he, Maggie and Philip become close (although after his recovery Tom distances himself from Philip again):

> After that, Philip spent all his time out of school-hours with Tom and Maggie. Tom listened with great interest to a new story of Philip's about a man who had a very bad wound in his foot, and cried out so dreadfully with the pain that his friends could bear with him no longer, but put him ashore on a desert island, with nothing but some wonderful poisoned arrows to kill animals with for food.
>
> 'I didn't roar out a bit, you know,' Tom said, 'and I dare say my foot was as bad as his. It's cowardly to roar.'
>
> But Maggie would have it that when anything hurt you very much, it was quite permissible to cry out, and it was cruel of people not to bear it. She wanted to know if Philoctetes had a sister, and why she didn't go with him on the desert island and take care of him. One day, soon after Philip had told this story, he and Maggie were in the study alone together while Tom's foot was being dressed [...] 'What are you reading about in Greek?' [Maggie] said. 'It's poetry, I can see

---

9   Josephine McDonagh, 'The Early Novels', in *The Cambridge Companion to George Eliot*, ed. by George Levine (Cambridge: Cambridge University Press, 2001), pp. 38–56 (53–54), https://doi.org/10.1017/ccol0521662672.003

that, because the lines are so short.' 'It's about Philoctetes, the lame man I was telling you of yesterday,' he answered, resting his head on his hand, and looking at her as if he were not at all sorry to be interrupted. Maggie, in her absent way, continued to lean forward, resting on her arms and moving her feet about, while her dark eyes got more and more fixed and vacant, as if she had quite forgotten Philip and his book. 'Maggie,' said Philip, after a minute or two, still leaning on his elbow and looking at her, 'if you had had a brother like me, do you think you should have loved him as well as Tom?' Maggie started a little on being roused from her reverie, and said, 'What?' Philip repeated his question. 'Oh, yes, better,' she answered immediately. 'No, not better; because I don't think I could love you better than Tom. But I should be so sorry,— so sorry for you.' Philip coloured; he had meant to imply, would she love him as well in spite of his deformity, and yet when she alluded to it so plainly, he winced under her pity.[10]

This sort of textual specificity, though, is not something carried systematically through the novel. Indeed elsewhere Eliot pokes mild fun at Tom's tutor, the Rev. Mr. Stelling, who 'was so broad-chested and resolute that he felt equal to anything' and who was certain he 'would by and by edit a Greek play, and invent several new readings. He had not yet selected the play, for having been married little more than two years, his leisure time had been much occupied with attentions to Mrs. Stelling; but he had told that fine woman what he meant to do some day, and she felt great confidence in her husband, as a man who understood everything of that sort'.[11] This is a mild poke at scholarship, of course, rather than tragedy as such, but it stages the larger issue: the Rev. Stelling's domestic duties, insofar as they come into conflict with his Attic ambition, take precedence. The novel, it turns out, is much more a domestic, private mode than it is a tragic, public one.

Early in *Mill* Eliot is explicit on precisely this matter. Young Tom and Maggie are entertaining their younger cousin, pretty little Lucy (who will go on, when grown-up, to plight her troth with handsome Stephen Guest). The kids are supposed to stay in the garden, but Tom wants to look at the pond and leads the two girls astray to see if they can find any water-snakes.

---

10   George Eliot, *Mill on the Floss* (Edinburgh: William Blackwood, 1860), book 2, ch. 6, https://www.gutenberg.org/files/6688/6688-h/6688-h.htm

11   Ibid., book 2, ch. 1.

'Here, Lucy!' he said in a loud whisper. Lucy came carefully as she was bidden, and bent down to look at what seemed a golden arrow-head darting through the water. It was a water-snake, Tom told her; and Lucy at last could see the serpentine wave of its body, very much wondering that a snake could swim. Maggie had drawn nearer and nearer; she must see it too, though it was bitter to her, like everything else, since Tom did not care about her seeing it. At last she was close by Lucy; and Tom, who had been aware of her approach, but would not notice it till he was obliged, turned round and said,–

'Now, get away, Maggie; there's no room for you on the grass here. Nobody asked you to come.' There were passions at war in Maggie at that moment to have made a tragedy, if tragedies were made by passion only; but the essential τι μέγεθος which was present in the passion was wanting to the action; the utmost Maggie could do, with a fierce thrust of her small brown arm, was to push poor little pink-and-white Lucy into the cow-trodden mud.[12]

The Greek, τι μέγεθος, means 'that greatness, magnitude' or 'necessary sublimity'. Eliot's point is that though little children may *feel* with heroic, or tragic, intensity, they can't *do* anything very much, and that means that their little dramas can never be properly tragic. And what Eliot considers true of children, scales in her telling to adults as well. We are not heroes, she says; we are ordinary, middling people. Tragedy does not describe our sorrow, even when that sorrow is very acute. Here is *Mill*'s narrator on the plight of Tom and Maggie's father, whose pride and obstinacy bring him to financial ruin, and takes somatic form in an apoplexy that leaves him bedridden.

Mr. Tulliver, you perceive, though nothing more than a superior miller and maltster, was as proud and obstinate as if he had been a very lofty personage, in whom such dispositions might be a source of that conspicuous, far-echoing tragedy, which sweeps the stage in regal robes, and makes the dullest chronicler sublime. The pride and obstinacy of millers and other insignificant people, whom you pass unnoticingly on the road every day, have their tragedy too; but it is of that unwept, hidden sort that goes on from generation to generation, and leaves no record,—such tragedy, perhaps, as lies in the conflicts of young souls, hungry for joy, under a lot made suddenly hard to them, under the dreariness of a home where the morning brings no promise with it, and where the unexpectant discontent of worn and disappointed parents

12   Ibid., book 1, ch. 10.

weighs on the children like a damp, thick air, in which all the functions
of life are depressed; or such tragedy as lies in the slow or sudden death
that follows on a bruised passion, though it may be a death that finds
only a parish funeral.[13]

Poor old Mr. Tulliver, who evokes in us neither pity nor any sort of
terror. Perhaps it's not that Thomas Gray's 'mute inglorious Milton' (to
quote his famous 'Elegy Written in a Country Graveyard') is denied his
public eloquence and glory by the mere happenstance of being born
into ordinary parochial life, but rather that ordinary parochialism
ontologically contradicts greatness *as such*—not that Gray's villager
might have written *Paradise Lost* if only things had gone a little different
for him, but rather that a Milton who doesn't speak gloriously isn't
Milton in any meaningful sense at all. Indeed, isn't it within the bounds
of possibility that Gray is celebrating, rather than lamenting, this silent
ingloriousness? The next line in his poem talks of Gray's parochial
Cromwell as guiltless of his country's blood. Surely it's better to be
laid in a country graveyard *without* blood on your hands than with?
(Pericles on his deathbed declared his proudest boast was that 'no
Athenian ever had to put on mourning because of me'.) Maybe it's not
the novel form, or even the larger social ethos, that makes tragedy such
an ill fit to Eliot's art. Maybe it's that the lines of force of her ethical
imagination are always tugging her out of drama as such, away from
the conflict, and towards something neither comic nor tragic but rather
a sense of the fundamental undisclosure of life as it is lived, and the
spiritual benefits of that state. Adam Mars-Jones says that 'mourning is a
wound that is also somehow an achievement'.[14] He wasn't talking about
tragedy when he said so, but he might as well have been. Tragic drama
stages mourning as a mode of ritualised social-religious sublimity,
parsing its shattering absences and ruptures into a sort of transcendent
achievement. But Eliot, however hard she tried to capture a Sophoclean
grandeur and depth in *The Mill on the Floss*, was working against the
grain of her genius. At her best she understands not that grief is not an
achievement, but rather that achievement itself is a kind of chimera, that
the best things we can do as human beings, things to do with kindness

---

13   Ibid., book 3, ch. 1.
14   Adam Mars-Jones, 'Chop, Chop, Chop', *London Review of Books*, 38.2 (2016), https://
     www.lrb.co.uk/the-paper/v38/n02/adam-mars-jones/chop-chop-chop

and connection and unobtrusiveness, are actually pointed, forceful, marvellous *un*achievements. When she writes novels—even when, as in this case, she writes a *tragic* novel—her aim is to capture the wisdom of the sort of being-in-the-world that evades the drama of tragedy and the melodramatic eventfulness of fiction.

At the end it is the river that is the uncertain quantity, flowing through a pastoral landscape for most of this novel only to rise up, a *deus ex machina* (or *deus ex fluvio*) to wrap-up the plot with preternatural abruptness. By the time she came to writing her greatest novel, *Middlemarch*, she knew better, and specified breaking the power of the river as a precondition for her heroine's happy blankness: Dorothea's energy 'like that river of which Cyrus broke the strength, spent itself in channels which had no great name on the earth. But the effect of her being on those around her was incalculably diffusive: for the growing good of the world is partly dependent on unhistoric acts; and that things are not so ill with you and me as they might have been, is half owing to the number who lived faithfully a hidden life, and rest in unvisited tombs'.[15] It's neither the first nor the last time this present study shall revert to these final lines of *Middlemarch*.

15　Eliot, *Middlemarch*, 'Finale'.

7. Epigraphy

Beginnings and Ends

It might be thought perverse, in a book explicitly about the use of epigraphs in *Middlemarch*, to have waited so long to quantify the specific lineaments of Eliot's epigraphy in the novel. There are, though, reasons why such work belongs at the end rather than the beginning. An epigraph precedes a chapter, of course; it comes at the beginning, or strictly speaking comes *before* the beginning. But we cannot make sense of the epigraph until we understand its relationship to the chapter it sets up, and we can only do that if we digest the whole chapter. So the epigraph which stands at the opening only makes sense at the close.

Middlemarch has eighty-seven chapters, but only eight-six epigraphs, since the 'finale' floats free of one. Thirteen of the novel's epigraphs are from Elizabethan/Jacobean dramatists;[1] and another fourteen are from Eliot's own pastiche versions of Elizabethan and Jacobean drama.[2] Twenty-one are from English poets, and another fourteen from Eliot's own pastiche verse in broad imitations of this tradition.[3] These two categories, real and pastiche drama from the age of Shakespeare, and real and pastiche English verse, constitute just under three quarters of all epigraphs. There are also eight epigraphs quoted from works of English

---

1   1, 11, 26, 32, 33, 36, 41, 42, 60, 66, 71, 77, 78; mostly William Shakespeare, but with some from Francis Beaumont and John Fletcher, Ben Jonson and Samuel Daniel.

2   4, 8, 9, 13, 18, 28, 31, 34, 43, 48, 55, 59, 64, 73.

3   The epigraphs to chapters 3, 12, 16, 21, 24, 25, 37, 39, 44, 50, 52, 56, 58, 62, 64, 68, 76, 80, 82, 83 and 84 are quoted variously from John Milton, Geoffrey Chaucer, Charles Sedley, Shakespeare's Sonnets, William Blake, Edmund Spenser, John Donne—credited as 'Dr Donne'—William Wordsworth, Henry Wotton, the anonymous author of the medieval ballad 'The Squyr of Lowe Degre', Daniel and the anonymous author of the fifteenth-century lyric 'The Not-Browne Mayde'. The epigraphs of Eliot's own 'pastiche' English verse head chapters 6, 14, 15, 17, 20, 23, 40, 47, 49, 51, 57, 67, 70 and 72.

     https://doi.org/10.11647/OBP.0249.07

prose fiction or non-fiction,[4] and five from various works of Continental prose fiction or non-fiction.[5] Six are quoted from Continental poets and two are 'proverbs' from the same provenance.[6] Two, only, are from the Bible [69, from Ecclesiasticus and 74 from Tobit]. Only one is an example of Eliot pastiche-ing English prose—chapter 53's 'It is but a shallow haste which concludeth insincerity from what outsiders call inconsistency—putting a dead mechanism of "ifs" and "therefores" for the living myriad of hidden suckers whereby the belief and the conduct are wrought into mutual sustainment'.[7]

What this points towards is Eliot marking her novel in terms of timbre. Roughly a third of epigraphs style their chapters—set them up, encourage us to read them—in terms of Elizabethan/Jacobean drama, and between a third and a half style their chapters via poetry. This is not quite to suggest that Eliot is obliquely teasing her reader on the level of tone, swapping the implication that this novel will turn out to be a tragedy, or that it will rather tend towards a poetic justice. It is, though, to present us with the lenses through which, if we choose, we can apprehend a finer-grained apprehension of the novel's achievement.

Consider, for example, the novel's very first chapter, and *Middlemarch*'s first epigraph.

---

4   5, 10, 29, 45, 61, 63, 79, 85; Robert Burton, Thomas Fuller, Oliver Goldsmith, Thomas Browne, Samuel Johnson and John Bunyan.

5   2, 30, 38, 75, 86; Miguel de Cervantes, Blaise Pascal, François Guizot and Victor Hugo.

6   19, 22, 27, 35, 54, 81; Dante, Alfred de Musset, Hesiod, Jean-François Regnard and Johann Wolfgang von Goethe. The epigraph for 7 is attributed to 'Italian proverb' and 46 to 'Spanish proverb'.

7   This sentiment, gussied into cod-seventeenth-century prose by Eliot, is not an uncommon one. 'There is such a power of what Mr. Lecky calls "localizing" principles and feelings, that a man will be indignant against this, or that form of a particular vice while he practises other forms of it without scruple. Such a man is flagrantly inconsistent; we should press the point of his inconsistency as a special argument to convince him, but we should not think of charging him with insincerity simply because he is inconsistent and imperfect. [...] To cases of mere inconsistency and imperfection, however glaring, it [the term *hypocrisy*] should not be applied at all. Strict hypocrisy, the conscious and deliberate pretence to virtues which a man has not and does not care to have, is, we suspect, much rarer than people commonly think'. 'Hypocrisy', *The Saturday Review* [1869], in *The Living Age*, ed. by E. Littell (Boston: Littell and Gay, 1869), vol. 103, pp. 279–81 (281), https://www.google. co.uk/books/edition/Littell_s_Living_Age/uKBIAQAAMAAJ?hl=en&gbpv=1

Since I can do no good because a woman,
Reach constantly at something that is near it.

—*The Maid's Tragedy*: BEAUMONT AND FLETCHER.

From here we move to a description of Dorothea: 'Miss Brooke had that kind of beauty which seems to be thrown into relief by poor dress'. It is an opening sentence that tells us two, linked things about Dorothea: that she is beautiful and that her beauty is of a particular sort, not over-obvious or showy, not dependent upon finery or make-up, but something plainer and purer. A beauty serious rather than trivial or frivolous. But we might argue that the epigraph has already positioned us to see that seriousness as severity, and perhaps even to expect violence.

The tangle of plot that constitutes *The Maid's Tragedy* hints at parallels with *Middlemarch* only to tug those parallels in unexpected directions. Aspatia (the titular maid) is in love with, and expects to marry, the noble Amintor; but the King instead decrees that Amintor must marry Evadne, supposedly to honour the fact that Evadne's brother, Melantius, has just won a famous military victory. Neither woman is happy about this development, and we might consider this a parallel, an invitation to read *Middlemarch* as a story about what happen when a young woman marries the wrong man. Aspatia and Evadne are not sisters, like Dorothea and Celia, and Evadne is compelled by exterior force rather than driven by her own spiritual and scholarly ambition, but the parallel is suggestive nonetheless. Then, however, we discover that the king has secretly forced Evadne to become his mistress, and is arranging the marriage to cover-up this sexual turpitude. Amintor, apprised of this state of affairs, does not sleep with his new bride and indeed, the King later instructs him *not* to have sex with Evadne, but to allow her to continue attending sexually upon the King at the royal pleasure. From here the play moves towards its bloody denouement: Amintor, Melantius and Evadne plan together to assassinate the king. The lines Eliot quotes come from a speech by Evadne, in conversation with Amintor positioned towards the end of Act 4. In it, she is full of self-loathing ('My whole life is so leprous, it infects/All my repentance').[8] He, bracingly, concurs: 'Can I believe/There's any seed of Vertue in that

---

8   Francis Beaumont and John Fletcher, *The Maid's Tragedy* (1619), https://www. gutenberg.org/cache/epub/10847/pg10847.html

woman[?] [...] O Evadne!/Would there were any safety in thy sex,/That I might put a thousand sorrows off,/And credit thy repentance: but I must not'. She begs him, abjectly, to forgive her:

> I do present my self the foulest creature,
> Most poysonous, dangerous, and despis'd of men,
> *Lerna* e're bred, or *Nilus*; I am hell,
> Till you, my dear Lord, shoot your light into me,
> The beams of your forgiveness.

...but Amintor cannot bring himself to do so, at least until Evadne speaks the monologue from which Eliot has extracted her epigraph.

> I have done nothing good to win belief,
> My life hath been so faithless; all the creatures
> Made for heavens honours have their ends, and good ones,
> All but the cousening Crocodiles, false women;
> They reign here like those plagues, those killing sores
> Men pray against; and when they die, like tales
> Ill told, and unbeliev'd, they pass away,
> And go to dust forgotten: But my Lord,
> Those short dayes I shall number to my rest,
> (As many must not see me) shall though too late,
> Though in my evening, yet perceive a will,
> Since I can do no good because a woman,
> Reach constantly at some thing that is near it;
> I will redeem one minute of my age,
> Or like another Niobe I'le weep till I am water.

Only after this does Amintor relent.

It is important to retain a sense of what Evadne is talking about here: namely, redeeming her sexual sinfulness by murdering the King—something she, indeed, presently goes off to do. Having tied the king to his bed and stabbed him to death, Evadne presents herself to Amintor, holding the knife she has used. She asks him to take her now, fully, as his wife. When he leaves the stage without making any such commitment she stabs *herself* to death. Returning to the stage to find her dying, Amintor then kills himself too.

This, frankly, is a very gnashing, bloody sort of context for the gentle easing-in of Eliot's pointedly unviolent novel. But a couple of things are likely to strike us, if we elect to look at the work through this magnifying lens. One is the way Evadne's speech anticipates, in a shamed and tragic voice, the celebrated *last* lines of *Middlemarch*, in which Dorothea too goes into a mode of storylessness, like, in Beaumont and Fletcher's words, a tale that is told, that 'pass[es] away,/And go[es] to dust forgotten'. Evadne is a crocodile-infested Nilus, where Dorothea is the forcefully flowing Tigris, broken into 360 channels, representative of the holy days of the antique calendar and therefore 'time' as such—as distinct from the temporal structures of textual narrative—by way of capturing how her singular will was diffused into quotidian duties and pleasures of the everyday.

> Her full nature, like that river of which Cyrus broke the strength, spent itself in channels which had no great name on the earth. But the effect of her being on those around her was incalculably diffusive: for the growing good of the world is partly dependent on unhistoric acts; and that things are not so ill with you and me as they might have been, is half owing to the number who lived faithfully a hidden life, and rest in unvisited tombs.[9]

The actual river is the Gyndes, a tributary of the Tigris. Eliot's reference here is to the account in Herodotus' *Histories* 1:189:

> The Gyndes rises in the hills of Matiene, and descending through the Dardonians, falls into the Tigris. While Cyrus was endeavouring to pass this same river, which might be crossed in ships, one of his sacred white horses boldly plunged into the stream, and attempted to swim over, but the stream having violently whirled it round, carried it away and drowned it. Cyrus, much offended with the river for this affront, threatened to render his stream so contemptible, that women should pass to either side without wetting their knees. After which menace, deferring his expedition against Babylon, he divided his army into two parts; and having marked out one hundred and eighty channels, by the line, on each side of the river, commanded his men to dig out the earth. His design was indeed executed by the great numbers he employed; but the whole summer was spent in the work. Thus Cyrus punished the river Gyndes, by draining the stream into three hundred and sixty trenches; and in the beginning of the next spring advanced with his army towards Babylon.[10]

---

9   Eliot, *Middlemarch*, 'Finale'.

10   Herodotus, *The History of Herodotus*, trans. by Isaac Littlebury (Oxford: W. Baxter, 1824), p. 73, https://www.google.co.uk/books/edition/The_History_of_Herodotus_Translated_By_I/XgPu0rLKGeIC?hl=en&gbpv=1

Nineteenth-century commentators agreed the rationale offered here was too thin to explain Cyrus's actions, since they delayed his war for a year. Explanation was divided between attempts at rationalisation—for instance, arguing that Herodotus records a garbled account of Cyrus's siege-craft, redirecting rivers in the attack on Babylon—and accounts that parse the account in *religious* or *mythic* terms (since white horses were sacred to the sun, and there were 360 days in the sacred year). It is likely Eliot was aware of both sides of this debate.

We need to return to the beginning of the novel, for we still have to navigate the pronounced divergence in tone, or mode, between Eliot's opening chapter and the grisly contextual implicature of the epigraph she chooses for it. The lines as quoted speak to the limitations that define female, as opposed to male, life, and acknowledge that such restrictions may have deleterious *moral* as well as practical consequences for actual women. If we assume that 'Since I can do no good because a woman [I will] reach constantly at something that is near it' means something bland and conventional, something like: prevented as I am by (as we would now say) structural sexism from achieving the fullest good, I will nonetheless try to do the best I can—then, perhaps, clicking the microscope lens into our instrument and examining the actual source will disabuse us. Evadne, here, is not saying that because perfect good is beyond her she will try to live as virtuously as she can. On the contrary, she is telling the man she loves, a man she has married despite being in a sexual relationship with another (married) man, that she will *murder* that other. The 'something near it' of virtue, in other words, is a miss as good as a mile.

Middlemarch does not tell the story of a marriage marred by a murderous wife of course, although it is a novel about a marriage in which the husband dies, unhappy in his heart with the fidelity of the woman he married, which is not a million miles from *A Maid's Tragedy*. Of course, it's possible all that's happening here is me attempting to over-leverage the significance of one short epigraph, merely because it stands at the head of the first chapter. But I don't think so. Look at the second sentence of that opening:

> [Dorothea's] hand and wrist were so finely formed that she could wear sleeves not less bare of style than those in which the Blessed Virgin appeared to Italian painters; and her profile as well as her stature and

bearing seemed to gain the more dignity from her plain garments, which by the side of provincial fashion gave her the impressiveness of a fine quotation from the Bible,—or from one of our elder poets,—in a paragraph of to-day's newspaper.[11]

In other words, Dorothea is not only beautiful, with that particular kind of refined beauty that is offset to advantage by plainness—she is *herself a quotation*, a particular sort of literary allusion, an epigraph in her own right. The other women of *Middlemarch* are workaday journalistic prose and she is a richer textual inset, a few lines from one of the poets Eliot herself so lavishly draws upon to augment and adorn her chapter headings. She is textual, because she is a character is a novel; but she is doubly textual, a more expressive or poetic 'text' than her companions. She stands out.

What Eliot is doing here is connecting this conceit, of Dorothea as an epigraph, to a related set of images to do with clothing, and more specifically with adornment. This brings into play another way of thinking of chapter epigraphs: as accessory. Clearly the main function of *Middlemarch* as a novel—the story, the characters, the descriptions and meditations—would be almost entirely unchanged if all the epigraphs were stripped out. They are not functional parts of the narrative, but rather they garnish, or adorn, the main text.

The novel's first interchange between Dorothea and her sister concerns them dividing up the jewels they have inherited from their dead mother. Dorothea agrees to this but qualifies herself by saying that 'we should never wear them, you know.' Celia replies that refusing to do so would indicate the girls 'are wanting in respect to mamma's memory', and Dorothea begins to soften her puritanism:

> The casket was soon open before them, and the various jewels spread out, making a bright parterre on the table. It was no great collection, but a few of the ornaments were really of remarkable beauty, the finest that was obvious at first being a necklace of purple amethysts set in exquisite gold work, and a pearl cross with five brilliants in it. Dorothea immediately took up the necklace and fastened it round her sister's neck, where it fitted almost as closely as a bracelet; but the circle suited the Henrietta-Maria style of Celia's head and neck, and she could see that it did, in the pier-glass opposite.

---

11   Eliot, *Middlemarch*, ch. 1.

'There, Celia! you can wear that with your Indian muslin. But this cross you must wear with your dark dresses.'

Celia was trying not to smile with pleasure. 'O Dodo, you must keep the cross yourself.'

'No, no, dear, no,' said Dorothea, putting up her hand with careless deprecation.

'Yes, indeed you must; it would suit you—in your black dress, now,' said Celia, insistingly. 'You might wear that.'

'Not for the world, not for the world. A cross is the last thing I would wear as a trinket.' Dorothea shuddered slightly.

'Then you will think it wicked in me to wear it,' said Celia, uneasily.

'No, dear, no,' said Dorothea, stroking her sister's cheek. 'Souls have complexions too: what will suit one will not suit another.'[12]

Souls have complexions too is a deft four-word summary of the work Eliot undertakes as a writer of fictional character. But this exchange not only establishes the differences in character of the sisters, it rehearses the place of epigraphs in the larger logic of the story. Are such quotations trinkets, trivialising the text, or adornments enriching it? The pearl-and-gemstone cross is too gaudy for Dorothea, but Celia wins her round, bringing out 'a fine emerald [ring] with diamonds' and comparing the sunlit jewels to the 'spiritual emblems in the Revelation of St. John'. Dorothea, persuaded, agrees to keep the ring and its accompanying bracelet ('All the while her thought was trying to justify her delight in the colours by merging them in her mystic religious joy'). So it is the type, not the fact, of epigraph that matters. And this returns us to the actual epigraphic choices Eliot has made. We might very well think that tragedy is serious enough, and poetry beautiful enough, to spiritually adorn the bald text, and so such quotations comprise three quarters of the whole.

Earlier I discussed something many critics have explored: the autobiographical contexts and resonances of *Mill on the Floss*. Less is made of these same contexts with respect to *Middlemarch*, although they are manifestly still there. Dorothea is beautiful where Marian Evans was ugly—ungallant of me to say so, I appreciate, but important, since this adventitious and fundamentally irrelevant fact had a major impact on her life possibilities. Dorothea's attraction to Casaubon, an older and more learned man, refracts a number of young Evans's relationships:

---

12   Ibid.

with R. H. Brabant, Herbert Spencer and John Chapman most notably. In life the possibility of actual emotional or erotic connection with these clever, older men was prevented by the plain fact of their being already married. But the affective truth of this repeating not-quite relationship pattern is, we can intuit, what informs *Middlemarch*: that intrinsic, not external, factors prevented their consummation. Consciously or otherwise George Eliot—the writer—knew what Marian Evans could not allow herself to see: not just that being in love with the intelligence and learning of a person is not the same being in love with a person (that much is so obvious it's almost facile to say so), but much more importantly that human desire is so constituted that it will cathect the former into the latter. Her love for literature, art, myth, the discourses of religion was so intense it carried itself through as much by eros as by agape and pragma, and in such a situation it's easy to fool oneself, or perhaps only to distract oneself from the inevitability of the counterpoint, that the eros encompasses the mentor, the teacher, the older man. It does not, of course, and *Middlemarch* is, amongst other things, Eliot explaining to Evans that it does not. Accordingly, Marian Evans's various affiliations with older scholars and editors, variously problematic, are here reinscribed as Dorothea actually marrying one such. And Marian Evans's eventual amatory redemption, with another married man, George Henry Lewes, is reworked as Dorothea's decision to flout both the disapproval of those older scholars and of society as a whole and to marry Ladislaw. Lewes was ugly and Ladislaw handsome, but the novel is entitled to balance out its unflinching emotional honesty with a little wish-fulfilment. As Marian Evans escaped Coventry to begin her life, so Dorothea escapes Middlemarch to begin hers.[13]

This is almost, but not quite, to suggest that *Middlemarch* is an autobiographical fiction. The point is not that Eliot has here written a *Prelude* or an *A la recherche du temps perdu*, for manifestly she hasn't. Nor has she written a *David Copperfield*, although this case is a little closer. As Charles Dickens inverts his name's CD into his protagonist's

---

13 That Dorothea is a fictionalised autobiographical self-portrait is an idea with a long history. It is, for instance, asserted in Isadore Gilbert Mudge and Minnie Earl Sears's *A George Eliot Dictionary: The Characters and Scenes of the Novels, Stories, and Poems Alphabetically Arranged* (London: Routledge & Sons, 1924). For a discussion of this, see Graham Handley's *George Eliot's Midlands: Passion in Exile* (London: Allison & Busby, 1991), pp. 15–40.

DC, so does he invert various aspects of his actual life—killing off his parents, inserting fairy tale elements (adding Betsey Trotwood as fairy godmother, strewing David's path with ogres and monsters, and finally winning his princess). The logic here is dream logic in a strict sense, which is to say, it undertakes the psychic work that Freud was interested in exploring. And, in fact, *Middlemarch* records a doubled inversion. On the one hand, beautiful Dorothea leaves Middlemarch just as plain Marian left Coventry (even the names invert one another: 'Dorothea' means 'given by God', and Mary is the woman who gave God). But on the other hand, plain Mary Garth does what plain Mary Ann never did: stays in Middlemarch, marries her love as a victory (that is: becomes a Vincy), has children and lives a fulfilled existence in the place she holds dear. Mary even becomes a published writer as Marian did, although this fantasy alternate George Eliot is defined by her sons and her *heimat*: a children's book, *Stories of Great Men, taken from Plutarch*, printed by the significantly named 'Gripp & Co., Middlemarch'. The main autobiographical 'fantasy' of Middlemarch is of a beautiful Marian Evans who leaves the claustrophobia of parochialism finally to begin her life with the handsome man she loves. Juxtaposed with this is a separate, smaller fantasy-autobiography: of the kind of woman Marian Evans actually was and could have stayed, gripping tight to her locale and putting her energies and love into her children.

I am aware, I hasten to add, of what Colin Burrow pithily calls 'the heuristic poverty of biographical explanations of works of art'.[14] My argument here is not that *Middlemarch* is autobiographical fiction, but on the contrary that, in a crucial sense, it isn't. Adam Phillips notes how hostile Freud was to biography as a whole. The mode is, he thought, structurally mendacious.

> We know that Freud, even as a younger man, didn't want a biography written about him; and that he is rather terrified (i.e. mocking) of his, perhaps presumptuously assumed, future biographers. It is equally evident that in writing about biographers and biographies he is writing about what he doesn't want psychoanalysts and psychoanalysis to be [...] When we speak about biography we speak about what we want lives, and life-stories, and truth-telling, to be.[15]

---

14   Colin Burrow, 'Who Wouldn't Buy It?', *London Review of Books*, 27.2 (2005), https://www.lrb.co.uk/the-paper/v27/n02/colin-burrow/who-wouldn-t-buy-it

15   Adam Phillips, *In Writing* (London: Penguin Books, 2019), p. 62.

Phillips's point is that 'for Freud, truth-telling about lives, such as it was, could be done only by the person himself, through the method of free-association, responded to by a psychoanalyst'. But he goes on to note, shrewdly, that 'yet, in some ways like the biographer, the analyst is giving the fragmentary discontinuous speech of the analysand a new narrative coherence. A new story is told out of an old story differently told'.

That's a good way of thinking of what Eliot has accomplished in *Middlemarch*: a new story being made out of an old story told differently. Quotation and epigraphy are linked ways of invoking old stories, of literally positioning markers to old stories into the body of the text; but Eliot uses both to remake and so build towards her new story. Her epigraphs (I've been arguing) are mirrors, which is to say, items of *mimesis*, encapsulations of literary realism. But I've also been arguing that they are lenses, which invokes a more complex mode of literary realism than is comprehended by more linearly reflective modes of what mimesis means. We are encouraged, throughout this novel, to look *through*, as well as to reflect (to reflect the beginning in the end, let's say). And amongst the things we are encouraged to look through is the kind of process of desiring a particular life-story that motivated Eliot herself.

It only looks trivialising—only appears facile—to talk of Dorothea as Marian Evans's 'wish-fulfilment' version of herself; because wish, or desire, is actually a much stranger and more complex dynamic than we generally think of it as being. We never really know why we want what we want. Indeed, we rarely know even *what* we want. We only know *that* we want. In such a condition (the human condition, the circumstance Freud spent his career excavating) we often misinvest our desire in wrongly-conceived or misapprehended targets. It's what both Dorothea and Lydgate do, after all (it's also what Casaubon does when he decides that marrying Dorothea is what he wants, but critics rarely talk about that). Indeed, their doing so is what gives this novel its extraordinary resonance with ordinary readers, because we all understand that something like this very often characterises our own desiring, and our own life-choices. In the case of George Eliot it doesn't, I think, take us too far into mere speculation to suggest that she both wanted a life somewhat like Dorothea's (to be beautiful, and spiritual, and adored by a handsome man she could adore, and most of all to *escape* parochial littleness) *and* a life like Mary Vincy's: rooted in a location she loved, surrounded by her own children. Rationally she knew she couldn't have both these things, but desire is not a rational process. This is a roundabout way of saying that what makes Eliot a great, rather than merely a proficient, novelist is her intuitive understanding not just that desire sabotages itself but that it is in this sabotage that art germinates. Dorothea does escape with the beautiful man she loves, but she publishes no books. Mary stays, and becomes a published writer, but a writer *for children*—Eliot's way of saying that Mary's story is of herself, of Marian Evans, *for* children, completed and sanctified by children. Mary takes the work of Plutarch, the most famous biographer of antiquity, perhaps the most famous biographer of all, and re-writes those biographies. She makes a new story out of an old story differently told. Both these fictionalised life-stories stand askew to the life-story of Marian Evans, plain, who did escape provincial littleness, who did become a published writer, who did not have children and did not, unlike her Ladislaw, George Henry Lewes, become a biographer.[16]

As we grow, and the reality principle intrudes increasingly upon our lives, we come to understand that it is infantile to believe we can always get what we want. In such a circumstance the reverse of this—that we can come, in time, to want what we get—perhaps looks like wisdom (hard-won, or otherwise); as it might be, the marriage of verity and wanting. But Eliot is interested in neither of these mutual-mappings of desire and lived-experience.

It seems to me both significant and characteristic of Eliot's strategy of intertextual allusion, that the last book named in *Middlemarch* (discounting Lydgate's unnamed 'treatise on Gout') is Plutarch's *Lives*, and that it appears not as itself but as reworked and retold. It is as a Freudian that Adam Phillips repeats Freud's belief 'that the best life stories are the ones told in psychoanalysis, in the psychoanalytic way. All other stories are rationalized self-deceptions'. But one need not be a

---

16   George Henry Lewes's first published book was *A Biographical History of Philosophy* (London: Charles Knight & Co., 1846) and he very often returned to biography across his writing career, as with *The Life of Maximilien Robespierre: With Extracts from his Unpublished Correspondence* (Philadelphia: Carey and Hart, 1849), *The Life and Works of Goethe* (London: David Nutt, 1855) and *Aristotle: A Chapter from the History of Science* (London: Smith, Elder & Co., 1864).

Freudian in any doctrinaire sense to agree that when an analyst is 'akin to a biographer, he is failing as a psychoanalyst'.

> The psychoanalytic method is, fortunately, easily explained. But we should note that there is no comparable biographical method. Nor is the biographer trying to cure anybody of anything; nor indeed is biography a mode of medical treatment.[17]

This study has spent some time considering the degree to which Eliot's 'realism' in *Middlemarch* is a *medical* realism. Biography, we might say, is realism raised to the level of realism: an exercise in *le naturalisme* from which the intermixture of fictional character is drained from the body of scrupulously recorded verisimilitude. But, of course, we wouldn't say anything so foolish: Freud is surely right that biography and autobiography both are rationalised self-deceptions. To get at the truth of a life, lived, means not recording verifiable exteriorities but, on the contrary, capturing interior myths and fantasies that are not only unverifiable, they are radically unfalsifiable too. At the end we come to understand the purpose of Eliot's epigraphy, and the underlying logic to her subtle, wide-ranging and eloquent intertextuality.

---

17   Phillips, *In Writing*, p. 56.

Postscript

The Flute inside the Bell

Middlemarch's thirty-first chapter opens with a conversation between Lydgate and Rosamond about Dorothea.

> Lydgate that evening spoke to Miss Vincy of Mrs. Casaubon, and laid some emphasis on the strong feeling she appeared to have for that formal studious man thirty years older than herself.
>
> 'Of course she is devoted to her husband,' said Rosamond, implying a notion of necessary sequence which the scientific man regarded as the prettiest possible for a woman; but she was thinking at the same time that it was not so very melancholy to be mistress of Lowick Manor with a husband likely to die soon. 'Do you think her very handsome?'
>
> 'She certainly is handsome, but I have not thought about it,' said Lydgate.
>
> 'I suppose it would be unprofessional,' said Rosamond, dimpling.[1]

There's quite a lot going on here, and it is not especially flattering to Lydgate. At the heart of this brief exchange are two different modes of cause-and-effect. Lydgate, 'the scientific man', assumes a 'billiard-ball striking another billiard-ball' model, a conception of necessary sequence. A woman agrees to marry a man. Ergo the woman loves the man. But Rosamond's 'of course' is not so mechanistic or sequential as this, and Eliot's point is that we, as readers, take the force of *her* rather than his understanding. Rosamond's 'of course' indexes social convention, not the motion of the heart, and stands-in for the material rather than the emotional satisfactions of the union. Not that Rosamond ignores the way actual desire, for a person rather than for social standing or material wealth, factors-in to human relationships. Her next statement,

---

1   Eliot, *Middlemarch*, ch. 31.

      https://doi.org/10.11647/OBP.0249.08

though styled as a question, actually figures by way of a mild accusation: 'you find her attractive, of course?' Lydgate's answer is, we presume, perfectly ingenuous: for his desire runs on rails in a way not true of his wife. His effective denial is then parried by Rosamond: *I suppose it would be unprofessional*, delivered with that tell-tale dimple, means: *naturally you desire her—for she is, as you have conceded, attractive—but you repress that desire for professional and socially-conventional reasons.*

Rosamond is over-reading her more simply constituted suitor, just as he is under-reading his more complexly constituted inamorata. It is a perfect encapsulation of their relationship, a more nuanced psychologically-grounded portrait of marital incompatibility than the one offered by Dorothea and Casaubon. In *their* case the mismatch is external, something the whole world can see; where Lydgate and Rosamond appear, to all external observers, to be very well matched indeed. That glint of steel in Rosamond's character implicit in 'it was not so very melancholy to be mistress of Lowick Manor with a husband likely to die soon' recruits empathy—for Rosamond is thinking herself into Dorothea's situation—to a materialist ruthlessness of feeling, and therefore of affect. It is a little thing that resonates significantly in terms of our understanding of Rosamond's character. Which is to say: it acts, as it were, epigraphically, smallness achieving a mode of largeness in the more capacious context of the novel as a whole.

The epigraph to this chapter is a piece of Eliotic verse:

> How will you know the pitch of that great bell
> Too large for you to stir? Let but a flute
> Play'neath the fine-mixed metal: listen close
> Till the right note flows forth, a silvery rill:
> Then shall the huge bell tremble—then the mass
> With myriad waves concurrent shall respond
> In low soft unison.

This versifies a phenomenon well-known to campanologists, and often discussed during this period.[2] Indeed, Eliot's little section of verse

---

2   'I was anxious to ascertain what relation the secondary tones of a large bell bore to its fundamental note, and for this purpose I availed myself of the excellent musical ear of my friend, Mr. Dodd, during his too short sojourn with me, and we went accompanied by a flute to the large bell of Salisbury Cathedral'. Charles Tomlinson, 'Mr Tomlinson's Experiments and Observations on Visible Vibration', *Records of General Science*, 2 (1835), 124–33 (p. 128).

describing this acoustic peculiarity was itself widely quoted and copied, especially in books about bell-ringing or acoustics.[3]

So widely quoted, in fact, did Eliot's short poem become that it began to be discussed on its own merits. Several commentators understood the passage in a theological sense, as (for instance) saying that our individual and mortal faith, though small in an absolute sense, might nonetheless resonate with the vastness of the Godhead.[4] More recently, Evan Horowitz has read the epigraph as being about 'social form'.[5] To read it as I propose here, as a more self-reflexive gesture on Eliot's part, a gloss as much on the realist novelist's apprehension of the nature of cause and effect in human character and interpersonal relation, is not to dismiss such takes, of course. Still, the epigraph in situ speaks more directly to questions of which effects are followed by causes, introducing the less obvious influences with the more direct hammer-strike—like Wallace Stevens's celebrated, if perhaps rather opaque, distinction

---

3   J. Solis Cohen's *The Throat and the Voice* (London: Ward, Lock, & Co., 1880) compares human vocalisation to campanological acoustics: 'Heavy bells are started by commencing with gentle impulses in rhythmic accord with the proper oscillation of the bell', adding: 'To quote from an excellent novel, *Middlemarch* ...' and citing the epigraph (p.123). The fifth chapter of Frank E. Miller's *The Voice* (New York: G. Schirmer, 1910), 'The Physiology and Psychology of Voice-Production', begins: 'Above this chapter I might well have placed the following lines which George Eliot wrote above Chapter XXXI of *Middlemarch* ...', then quoting the epigraph (p.180). The anonymously authored article on 'The Bell' in *The Southern Review*, 22 (1877), 372, follows a lengthy prose account of campanological acoustics with the words: 'this is matter-of-fact prose, dealing with bells in the rough. Now listen to this perfect poetry from George Eliot, which by its magic touch transforms the bell into a thing of life', quoting the lines.

4   For example, the unsigned article in *The Bible Christian Magazine*, 17 (1881), 60 that quotes Eliot's lines and adds: 'thus the slightest touch of faith makes the nature of the Godhead quiver to the centre'. Joseph William Reynolds's *The Mystery of the Universe, Our Common Faith* (London: Kegan Paul, 1884), p. 274 and Henry Burton's *The Gospel According to St. Luke* (New York: A.C. Armstrong and Son, 1893), p. 74 both quote these lines, to similar purpose.

5   'If it is not immediately clear that these lines are about social form, rather than, say, the acoustics of bells, the evidence is nonetheless there—most directly in that pointed word "mass", and most profoundly in the final cadence, where the "mass" is made a chorus of individuals singing in "low soft unison."' Evan Horowitz, 'Industrialism and the Victorian Novel'. Evan Horowitz, 'Industrialism and the Victorian Novel', in *The Oxford Handbook of the Victorian Novel*, ed. by Lisa Rodensky (Oxford: Oxford University Press, 2013), https://www.oxfordhandbooks.com/view/10.1093/oxfordhb/9780199533145.001.0001/oxfordhb-9780199533145-e-021373. The moral he draws is: 'though the whole of society may seem overgrown or unwieldy, the right cause, the right ideal, the right note will show its resounding harmony.'

between the beauty of inflections and the beauty of innuendoes.[6] We are, according to the idiom 'struck' by another person's beauty, like a bell being struck by its clapper. Rosamond and Dorothea are both beautiful, and Lydgate is struck by both; but, considered in terms of cause and effect, one has a more insinuating, resonant effect upon him than the other. Why might this be? To answer such questions we turn, perhaps, to the character, perhaps even the subconscious subjectivities of the individual effected; but to do so in this context is to realise how rich the ironies of Eliot's characterisation are. Lydgate, who believes in a simple chain of cause-and-effect, is actually to be acted upon with a more flute-line trembling. What we feel we ought to desire and what we actually desire rarely align.

That this is so is picked out in the chapter's eighth paragraph, following this brief and flirtatious exchange from Lydgate's courting of Rosamond. Before he leaves, Lydgate lifts and smells Rosamond's perfumed handkerchief 'as if to enjoy its scent' (why *as if*? Is Eliot hinting at a less self-evident motive?) The narrator continues:

> But this agreeable holiday freedom with which Lydgate hovered about the flower of Middlemarch, could not continue indefinitely. It was not more possible to find social isolation in that town than elsewhere, and two people persistently flirting could by no means escape from 'the various entanglements, weights, blows, clashings, motions, by which things severally go on.'

The line quoted is neither identified in the text, nor is its provenance particularly obvious.[7] It is, though, germane to this question of human motivation, of cause and effect, that is shaping Lydgate's personal, and the novel's collective, narrative. The quotation is Lucretian, from a section of the *De Rerum Natura* describing how the primal nature of matter as a 'state of discord' led to all the atoms in the universe 'joining battle, disordered their interspaces, passages, connexions, weights,

---

6   For a still valuable investigation of nineteenth-century literature—though not, specifically, of Eliot—under this aegis, see Jerome J. McGann's *The Beauty of Inflections: Literary Investigations in Historical Method and Theory* (Oxford: Clarendon Press, 1985).

7   Its source evades the editorial labour of Bert G. Hornback in his 'Norton Critical Edition' of the novel (Scranton, PA: W. W. Norton & Co., 1977), although David Carroll correctly identifies it in his Oxford edition (Oxford: Oxford University Press, 1997).

blows, clashings, motions, because by reason of their unlike forms and varied shapes they could not all remain thus joined together nor fall into mutually harmonious motions'.[8] It is, of course, a radically materialist vision of the universe, although Lucretius's actual account of cause-and-effect is rather more nuanced and complex than is sometimes assumed.[9] If Lydgate were to take fully to heart the implications of living in this clashing tempest of interactions he would, we can presume, be less complacent. There's a leaven of humour here too, of course: describing this one Midlands town in the 1830s in terms of a cosmic downpour of clashing Lucretian atoms. But it touches on something that some critics of Eliot have argued persuasively: that one of her distinctive attributes as a writer is precisely her repudiation of linear cause and effect.[10]

To return to Eliot's epigraphic bell: the particular phraseology in this short piece of verse is significant. Blow upon your flute, under the giant metal structure, and 'the mass/With myriad waves concurrent shall respond/In low soft union'. That word—concurrent—is an important one for *Middlemarch*. It first occurs during an exchange between Bulstrode and Lydgate, indicative of the difference in their respective world-views.

> 'I am aware,' [Bulstrode] said, 'that the peculiar bias of medical ability is towards material means. Nevertheless, Mr. Lydgate, I hope we shall not vary in sentiment as to a measure in which you are not likely to be actively concerned, but in which your sympathetic concurrence may be an aid to me. You recognize, I hope; the existence of spiritual interests in your patients?'
>
> 'Certainly I do. But those words are apt to cover different meanings to different minds.'[11]

---

8   This is H. A. J. Munro's translation, *De Rerum Natura Libri Sex*, 2 vols (Cambridge: Deighton Bell & Co., 1866), vol. 2, p. 126. The Latin is: *discordia quorum/intervalla vias conexus pondera plagas/concursus motus turbabat proelia miscens/propter dissimilis formas variasque figuras,/quod non omnia sic poterant coniuncta manere* [*De Natura Rerum*, 5:436–38].

9   See, for instance, David Webb 'On Causality and Law in Lucretius and Contemporary Cosmology', in *Contemporary Encounters with Ancient Metaphysics*, ed. by Abraham Jacob Greenstine and Ryan J. Johnson (Edinburgh: Edinburgh University Press, 2017), pp. 254–69.

10   See, for instance, Sally Shuttleworth's reading of *Daniel Deronda* as a novel demonstrating Eliot's rejection of 'a linear sequence of cause and effect [...] full authoritative knowledge, she asserts, cannot be obtained by tracing through a linear sequence of cause and effect'. Sally Shuttleworth, *George Eliot and Nineteenth-Century Science: The Make-Believe of a Beginning* (Cambridge: Cambridge University Press, 1984), p. 177.

11   Eliot, *Middlemarch*, ch. 13.

Sympathetic concurrence, here, mediates between Bulstrode's spiritual apprehension of the universe and the physical, Lucretian connections of Lydgate's materialism. The word appears again at the meeting Bulstrode chairs to determine whether the 'scientific' Vicar Farebrother or the more conventionally religious Tyke ('a man entirely given to his clerical office') be given the lucrative position of secretary at the new hospital—Tyke, of course, being Bulstrode's man:

> Lydgate was late in setting out, but Dr. Sprague, the two other surgeons, and several of the directors had arrived early; Mr. Bulstrode, treasurer and chairman, being among those who were still absent. The conversation seemed to imply that the issue was problematical, and that a majority for Tyke was not so certain as had been generally supposed. The two physicians, for a wonder, turned out to be unanimous, or rather, though of different minds, they concurred in action.[12]

The Doctor is 'more than suspected of having no religion' by Middlemarch society—though this fact is not held against him ('it is certain that if any medical man had come to Middlemarch with the reputation of having very definite religious views, of being given to prayer, and of otherwise showing an active piety, there would have been a general presumption against his medical skill'). He and his colleagues concur in preferring the more scientific Farebrother. Lydgate, though it makes him wince to be believed to be kowtowing to Bulstrode—and although Farebrother is his friend—votes for Tyke. His anxieties have some grounding in reality. 'Mr. Wrench and Mr. Toller', the narrator says, 'were just now standing apart and having a friendly colloquy, in which they agreed that Lydgate was a jackanapes, just made to serve Bulstrode's purpose'. But this passage goes on to point up the mild social hypocrisy of these gentlemen, for 'to non-medical friends they had already concurred in praising the other young practitioner'. *Concurrence*, once again, speaks not to harmonious unanimity but rather to more practically-minded compromises.

The next use of the word is again associated with Lydgate: this time chapter 30's interview between the doctor and Dorothea over Casaubon's failing health. Informing her that Casaubon 'may possibly live for fifteen years or more, without much worse health than he has had hitherto', at which news 'Dorothea had turned very pale, and when Lydgate paused

---

12   Ibid., ch. 18.

she said in a low voice, "You mean if we are very careful"'. Her point is that 'he would be miserable if he had to give up his work' and Lydgate's reply is less lucid than it first seems:

'I am aware of that. The only course is to try by all means, direct and indirect, to moderate and vary his occupations. With a happy concurrence of circumstances, there is, as I said, no immediate danger from that affection of the heart, which I believe to have been the cause of his late attack. On the other hand, it is possible that the disease may develop itself more rapidly: it is one of those cases in which death is sometimes sudden. Nothing should be neglected which might be affected by such an issue.'[13]

The 'happy concurrence' to which Lydgate here refers is a notional congeries of eventualities that will, somehow, protect Casaubon's fragile heart.

As the story goes on, Bulstrode's interference in the management of the hospital threatens to sink it (the narrator speaks of 'the outburst of professional disgust at the announcement of the laws Mr. Bulstrode was laying down for the direction of the New Hospital, which were the more exasperating because there was no present possibility of interfering with his will and pleasure'),[14] Lydgate gives up part of his practice to be able to devote more time to the project ('I must work the harder, that's all, and I have given up my post at the Infirmary') and Bulstrode assures him: 'Mr. Brooke of Tipton has already given me his concurrence, and a pledge to contribute yearly: he has not specified the sum—probably not a great one'. This *concurrence* is a fancy way of saying: he has agreed to give me some money (though not much money)—the pun on *currency* is right there—and marks a further debasement on what 'concurrent' might signify. Money also haunts the next connection of Lydgate with concurrence. During Rosamond's post-miscarriage convalescence Lydgate finds himself 'unable to suppress all signs of inward trouble', and as her health recovers he meditates 'taking her entirely into confidence on his [financial] difficulties'. There are too many tradesmen's bills, and they need to retrench financially: but 'how could such a change be made without Rosamond's concurrence?'.[15] By the time we get to chapter 71's

13   Ibid., ch. 30.
14   Ibid., ch. 45.
15   Ibid., ch. 58.

account of Bulstrode's downfall it is no surprise to see the same word utilised. Hawley addresses the meeting:

> In what I have to say, Mr. Chairman, I am not speaking simply on my own behalf: I am speaking with the concurrence and at the express request of no fewer than eight of my fellow-townsmen, who are immediately around us. It is our united sentiment that Mr. Bulstrode should be called upon—and I do now call upon him—to resign public positions which he holds not simply as a tax-payer, but as a gentleman among gentlemen.[16]

This concurrence is a collective outflanking, and marks the end of Bulstrode. The other bigwigs of Middlemarch are running together, as a pack (the Latin *concurro* has the primary meaning 'I run with others, I flock', and only subsequently came to mean 'I concur, I coincide': *curro* means 'I run'). If *currency* is one punning association of concurrence, the canine or lupine *curs* is another. Wolves; people; money.

It says little to note that Eliot 'runs together' her storylines. We could say the same about most writers. But Eliot has a closer eye than most to the way 'running-together' is both a kind of *currency* and a kind of influence—not a billiard ball striking another, but a more subtle penetration of influence from individual to individual. It is to create a whole world through the creation of a single flute-note, by sounding your finer instrument inside the canopy of the bell. Currency means money (hospitals don't run without money; younger relatives' debts aren't quitted without money; wives with expensive tastes aren't satisfied without it). Currency also means contemporaneity ('current affairs'), a more complicated relationship for this novel set pre-Darwin but very much written by a sensibility formed post-. And, to return to the beginning of this chapter, there's a particular, quasi-musical concurrence chiming, or sounding, through this novel.

Bells summon the faithful to church, and summon children to school, which is to say: they are instruments of congregation. In chapter 77 the widowed Dorothea on the pretext of attending to the donation of a bell to a school, calls on Lydgate—this at the time of collective suspicion regarding his closeness to the disgraced Bulstrode—hoping to reassure him. Her mind is also running on her burgeoning love for Ladislaw. This 'fine-toned bell'—

---

16   Ibid., ch. 71.

Dorothea had another errand in Lowick Gate: it was about a new fine-toned bell for the school-house, and as she had to get out of her carriage very near to Lydgate's, she walked thither across the street, having told the coachman to wait for some packages.[17]

—leads to an unexpected congregation:

She found herself on the other side of the door without seeing anything remarkable, but immediately she heard a voice speaking in low tones which startled her as with a sense of dreaming in daylight, and advancing unconsciously a step or two beyond the projecting slab of a bookcase, she saw, in the terrible illumination of a certainty which filled up all outlines, something which made her pause, motionless, without self-possession enough to speak.

Seated with his back towards her on a sofa which stood against the wall on a line with the door by which she had entered, she saw Will Ladislaw: close by him and turned towards him with a flushed tearfulness which gave a new brilliancy to her face sat Rosamond, her bonnet hanging back, while Will leaning towards her clasped both her upraised hands in his and spoke with low-toned fervour.

'Dorothea', says Eliot, 'after the first immeasurable instant of this vision' retreats. She 'walked across the street with her most elastic step and was quickly in her carriage again'. The shock of the encounter, the vibration of this suspicion, is described by Eliot in terms of a crowd, a 'throng' ('she had seen something so far below her belief, that her emotions rushed back from it and made an excited throng without an object'), or as she later says when her sister intuits she is upset, a global population: in reply to Celia's question 'has something happened?', Dorothea asserts that 'a great many things have happened [...] all the troubles of all people on the face of the earth'. This abrupt erosion of lover's faith is another kind of concurrence.

That it proves a misunderstanding does nothing to defang this moment, a kind of second disappointment, or loss of innocence, for Dorothea. The failure of her marriage to Casaubon indexed her own naivety (for Casaubon was always exactly what he seemed to be); but this hints that her love for Ladislaw might have fixed itself on an inconstant and unworthy object. A few chapters later these feelings are renewed, and again Eliot connects it to the bell. At a loose end, and somewhat agitated, Dorothea

---

17   Ibid., ch. 77.

walked straight to the schoolhouse and entered into a conversation with
the master and mistress about the new bell, giving eager attention to
their small details and repetitions, and getting up a dramatic sense that
her life was very busy.[18]

From here to the parsonage, where Dorothea's agitation is increased
by the guileless Miss Noble, who has a 'German box', a present from
Ladislaw, and whose ardent feelings are the subject of jolly gossip.

> 'If Henrietta Noble forms an attachment to any one, Mrs. Casaubon,' said
> [Farebrother's] mother, emphatically,—'she is like a dog—she would
> take their shoes for a pillow and sleep the better.'
>   'Mr. Ladislaw's shoes, I would,' said Henrietta Noble.
>   Dorothea made an attempt at smiling in return. She was surprised
> and annoyed to find that her heart was palpitating violently, and that
> it was quite useless to try after a recovery of her former animation.
> Alarmed at herself—fearing some further betrayal of a change so marked
> in its occasion, she rose and said in a low voice with undisguised anxiety,
> 'I must go; I have overtired myself.'[19]

That's another function of a bell, of course: as with the tolling bell of
Donne's 'no man is an island' sermon, it recalls us to our mortality, or,
in Dorothea's case, the death of her hopes. That these late misdirections
are linked by Eliot to Dorothea's school bell is a mild irony. We could
say: its chime is schooling her in the depth, and precarity, of her own
feelings. Her grief after her visit to the priory rings her like a bell: '"Oh,
I did love him!" Then came the hour in which the waves of suffering
shook her too thoroughly to leave any power of thought'. Sound waves,
emotional waves, passing out and influencing the world.

   This flute-note concurrency is illustrated by the scene that follows,
in which Dorothea goes to Rosamond to 'save' her—that is, to dissuade
her from having an affair with Ladislaw—and Rosamond, intuiting
the direction in which her delicately circumlocutionary phraseology is
going, steps in when the words stop coming. The moment is articulated
in terms not only of mutual vibration, a spontaneous concurrency of
feeling that leads to intimacy, but also of what the epigraph to chapter
31, with which *this* chapter began, calls 'a low soft unison':

> The waves of her own sorrow, from out of which she was struggling to
> save another, rushed over Dorothea with conquering force. She stopped

18   Ibid., ch. 80.
19   Ibid.

in speechless agitation, not crying, but feeling as if she were being inwardly grappled. Her face had become of a deathlier paleness, her lips trembled, and she pressed her hands helplessly on the hands that lay under them. Rosamond, taken hold of by an emotion stronger than her own—hurried along in a new movement which gave all things some new, awful, undefined aspect—could find no words, but involuntarily she put her lips to Dorothea's forehead which was very near her, and then for a minute the two women clasped each other as if they had been in a shipwreck. 'You are thinking what is not true,' said Rosamond, in an eager half-whisper.[20]

How *will* you know the pitch of that great bell/Too large for us to stir? Breathe upon your flute, and listen close/Till the right note flows forth, a silvery rill:

> Then shall the huge bell tremble—then the mass
> With myriad waves concurrent shall respond
> In low soft unison.

I have one last observation with respect to the six-and-a-half lines of Eliot's bell verse. The relative eclipse of reputation of Friedrich Schiller— in Britain, I mean—between the nineteenth-century and the present day occludes the most obvious intertext for Eliot's short 'bell' poem: Schiller's lengthy 'Das Lied von der Glocke' (1798). Eliot, a dedicated reader of Schiller, was certainly aware of this 'Song of the Bell'.[21] Schiller traces the life of the bell from raw materials, through its casting to its transportation and hanging—this a collective activity, *Tausend fleißge Hände regen/helfen sich in munterm Bund*, 'a thousand hands, busy in motion, help in cheerful union'—until the bell is finally sounded, and named 'CONCORDIA', whose chime brings all people's together, and sings-out with a star-bright sound:

---

20 Ibid., ch. 81.
21 'As Mary Sibree, to whom she taught German, records it: 'Placing together one day the works of Schiller [. . .] Miss Evans said, "Oh, if I had given these to the world, how happy I should be!"' (Cross, p. 53). Although her reading of Schiller was at its most intense in the early 1840s, the 'thrill' she felt at the sight of his house in Weimar in 1854, as well as references to him as late as in *Middlemarch* and *Daniel Deronda*, show that her attraction to his work remained strong throughout her life. The impact of his work on her own is considerable'. Deborah Guth, 'George Eliot and Schiller: Narrative Ambivalence in *Middlemarch* and *Felix Holt*', *Modern Language Review*, 94.4 (1999), 913–24 (p.). See also Guth's book-length study, *George Eliot and Schiller: Intertextuality and Cross-Cultural Discourse* (Surrey: Ashgate Publishing, 2003).

> *Soll eine Stimme sein von oben,*
> *Wie der Gestirne helle Schar!*

This joyous, ingenuous peroration to the 'unison' that Eliot's bell also sounds is one of Schiller's most famous poems. Even more famous is his essay *Über naive und sentimentalische Dichtung* (1795–96), 'On Naïve and Sentimental Poetry'.[22] And it has sometimes seemed to me that Eliot's novel sets out, playfully enough but with a serious purpose for all that, to upend Schiller's distinction. We could put it this way: Dorothea at the beginning of *Middlemarch* is naïve, whereas at the end, as she realises how easily her sensibility—her genuine love for Ladislaw—could capsize her, she becomes sentimental. But her naivety is not a Schillerian unity of subject and object; it is, on the contrary, an intensely self-considered, self-conscious setting of herself a goal for her life, where her sentimentality is so spontaneous that it eventually moves her, and the object of her love, out of the artificiality of the fiction that is *Middlemarch* altogether. In *The Book on Adler* (1872), Søren Kierkegaard claims that 'though it is indeed by writing that one justifies the claim to be an author, it is also, strangely enough, by writing that one virtually renounces this claim. To find the conclusion it is necessary first of all to observe that it is lacking, and then in turn to feel quite vividly the lack of it'.[23] The coming-together of Dorothea and Ladislaw feels to some

---

22   German original available at http://www.zeno.org/Literatur/M/Schiller,+Friedrich/ Theoretische+Schriften/%C3%9Cber+naive+und+sentimentalische+Dichtung. James Wood prefers 'simple' as an Englishing of the German *naive*: 'Schiller argues that the ancient writers, especially the Greeks, were at one with nature, combining thought and feeling, while the modern writer can only seek or aspire to nature, worshipping or elegising what he no longer possesses simply. Schiller finds in the Greeks "a character of calm necessity. Their impatient imagination only traverses nature to pass beyond it to the drama of human life." The modern poet, by contrast, is always sentimental about nature, like a sick man yearning for health. Indeed, the sentimental poet idealises nature much as we (including, self-confessedly, Schiller) sentimentalise the Greeks themselves. The problem for modern literature of this loss of innocence is that, in contrast with the ancient simple poet, we never see "the object itself": instead, the modern poet is always reflecting on the impressions he receives from nature, always "a spectator of his own emotion". Schiller's examples of simple poets are Homer and Shakespeare; of sentimental poets, Milton and Kleist'. James Wood, 'Buckets of Empathy', *London Review of Books*, 22.7 (2000), https://www.lrb.co.uk/the-paper/v22/n07/james-wood/buckets-of-empathy

23   Søren Kierkegaard, *On Authority and Revelation: The Book on Adler, or a Cycle of Ethico-Religious Essays*, trans. by Walter Lowrie (Princeton: Princeton University Press, 1955), p. 65.

readers like a conclusion as well as a consummation, but Eliot is canny enough to understand that it actually represents the lack—the rather vivid lack—of a conclusion. Or to put it another way: a hammer strike meeting the bell's metal might be simple, but there is more haunting and spiritual unison in the flute-song, sentimental though it be, inside the bell's hood.

A bell is revealed as—if this isn't too bizarre a way of putting it— an auditory mirror: our action upon it, direct or inferential, is bounced back resonantly to us. The chiming of bells is a preliminary, a kind of aural epigraph, to a church service; and a short text, an epigraph, is the verbal preliminary to the sermon at the heart of the service. Such items stand not as models of the larger, or longer, work to which they append themselves so much as fractal *ratio minores*, encapsulations that reflect, like the drop of ink at the end of the pen with which Eliot opens *Adam Bede*. We can see in them, and through them, and what we can see are the vistas Eliot's great novel opens to us.

It would, however, be perverse to end a study that proposes to read Eliot's novel via mirrors and lenses with a bell. After all, *Middlemarch* is not lacking in deictic pointers to its own specular design. This is how chapter 27 opens:

> An eminent philosopher among my friends,[24] who can dignify even your ugly furniture by lifting it into the serene light of science, has shown me this pregnant little fact. Your pier-glass or extensive surface of polished steel made to be rubbed by a housemaid, will be minutely and multitudinously scratched in all directions; but place now against it a lighted candle as a centre of illumination, and lo! the scratches will seem to arrange themselves in a fine series of concentric circles round that little sun. It is demonstrable that the scratches are going everywhere impartially and it is only your candle which produces the flattering illusion of a concentric arrangement, its light falling with an exclusive optical selection. These things are a parable. The scratches are events, and the candle is the egoism of any person now absent—of Miss Vincy, for example.

---

24 It is tricky to prove, but nonetheless likely, that the 'eminent friend' referred to here was scientist William Edward Ayrton (1847–1908), who lectured to the Royal Society on mirrors and electric illumination, and was involved in a number of advances in arc-lights, electrical communication and other things. Eliot befriended Ayrton's daughter Hertha in the early 1870s, and helped her gain a place at Girton.

This 'parable' has been widely discussed by Eliot's critics, although given how assiduously Eliot herself spells-out its meaning, elaboration runs the risk of being supererogatory. For J. Hillis Miller, the crucial thing here is the way Eliot describes her own mimetic mirror-work, as novelist, in parabolic terms: as the 'parable' lays clear the lines of sight that are gathered, on parabolic trajectories, by this mirror.[25] Barbara Leckie, with perhaps greater penetration into Eliot's craft, focuses instead on the way her mimetic reflectivity is *augmented* (rather than, as we might think, compromised) by the 'cross-hatching of scratches' here identified: 'the cross-hatching of scratches also signal one of the novel's central organising motifs: the web. That is, the pier glass is at once a reflective surface and a surface that invokes a web; it represents the mirror not as a straightforward reflection but rather, as Leah Price puts it, "the mirror as a system of infinite connections"'.[26] It is a web, and a bell, and both are in some sense a mirror—the mimetic art in which a small, distorted thing reflects back to us the large, beautiful thing.

The chapter with which this passage opens *pre*-begins with this epigraph:

> Let the high Muse chant loves Olympian:
> We are but mortals, and must sing of man.

This is Eliot's translation of the following two lines from Theocritus:

> Μοῦσαι μὲν θεαὶ ἐντί, θεοὺς θεαὶ ἀείδοντι:
> ἄμμες δὲ βροτοὶ οἵδε, βροτοὺς βροτοὶ ἀείδωμεν.[27]

A more literal rendering might go: 'the Muses, though, are gods and being gods do sing of gods; we who are here (οἵδε) are mortals, and as mortals let us sing of mortals.' Eliot loses something by condensing the

---

25 '"Parable" means, etymologically, "thrown beside," from the Greek *para*, beside, and *ballein*, to throw. A parable is set or thrown at some distance from the meaning which controls it and to which it obliquely or parabolically refers, as, in its definition, a parabolic curve is controlled, across a space, by its parallelism to a line on the cone of which it is a section [...] the parabola creates that line in the empty air, just as the parables of Jesus remedy a defect of vision, give sight to the blind, and make the invisible visible'. Joseph Hillis Miller, *Reading for Our Time: Adam Bede and* Middlemarch *Revisited* (Edinburgh: Edinburgh University Press, 2012), p. 65.

26 Barbara Leckie, *Open Houses: Poverty, the Novel, and the Architectural Idea in Nineteenth-Century Britain* (Philadelphia: University of Pennsylvania Press, 2018), p. 191, https://doi.org/10.9783/9780812295177

27 Theocritus, *Idylls*, 16:3–4.

thrice-repeated θεαὶ (goddesses) and thrice-repeated βροτός (mortal men) that balance it, not least the gender distinction between female goddesses and mortal men.

Theocritus's poem turns out to be about how far men have fallen (into love of money and other things) and yet how it remains possible that they can be redeemed, and open their houses to the Χάριτες— the 'Graces': Aglaea ('Shining'), Euphrosyne ('Joy') and Thalia ('Blooming'). Grace (Χάρις) has an important place in Christian thought, of course; as do 'parables'. And Theocritus's poem says that *though* we are broken, scratched as in Eliot's 'parable' of the mirror, grace can still enter in. It is hard not to wonder if Eliot, by invoking this gracious poem, is not inviting us to see rose-blooming Rosamond as Thalia, spiritually-illuminated Dorothea as Aglaea and, smaller than the other two in terms of the space the novel allows her, but surely just as important in terms of what she says about the lineaments of female happiness, quietly joyful Mary Garth as Euphrosyne.

And even this, I would say, modest unpacking of a particular epigraph entails the lensing, or flute-resonance, that Eliot's epigraphs so often do. Her choices as a translator, by de-gendering and de-repetitising a gendered, triply-insistent original, universalise and render less insistently rhetorical the underlying sentiment. Most of all, by translating the original triad of Muse-Graces as a single 'Muse', Eliot gestures, delicately enough, at the unifying vision she is attempting in her novel.

Here, for comparison, is a roughly-contemporaneous Victorian translation of the opening lines of Theocritus's sixteenth idyll:

> This is ever a care to the daughters of Jove, ever to poets, to hymn immortals, to hymn the glories of brave men. The Muses indeed are goddesses; goddesses sing of gods: but we are mortals here; let us mortals sing of mortals. Yet who of as many as dwell under the bright dawn, will open his doors, and graciously welcome in his home our Graces, and not send them away again unrewarded?[28]

The translator here adds a footnote, glossing Χάριτες as 'i.e. his poems. For a similar prosopopoeia see Horace's Epistle 1:20 where he compares

---

28   'Idyll XVI: The Graces; Or, Hiero', *The Idylls of Theocritus, Bion and Moschus, and the War-songs of Tyrtaeus*, trans. by Rev. J. Banks (London: George Bell and Sons, 1878), p. 84.

his book with a damsel desiring to go forth in public'. Theocritus's poem, in other words, is a poem about poetry, a self-reflexive text, not in a hermetically sealed or inward manner but, on the contrary, in the sense that poetry goes out into the world. Eliot's novel, similarly, refracts its textualities dialectically between epigraph-small and chapter-, and novel-, large. This specular epigraphy is a line of sight that combines the microscopic and the telescopic, that shines upon the mirror's scratches in order not to overlook or occlude them but rather to transform them in the brilliancy of Eliot's imaginative reconfiguration into something as beautiful as true. That *Middlemarch* is a novel that balances the small and the large is hardly a new critical observation of course. Back in 1975, J. Hillis Miller argued that Eliot's configures *Middlemarch* such that

> a fragment is examined as a 'sample' of the larger whole of which it is a part, though the whole impinges on the part as the 'medium' within which it lives, as national politics affect Middlemarch when there is a general election, or as the coming of the railroad upsets rural traditions. Eliot's strategy of totalization is to present individual character or event in the context of that wider medium and to affirm universal laws of human behavior in terms of characters.[29]

This strikes me as both an over-emphasis on 'totalization' as Eliot's aesthetic strategy, and an over-emphasis on such in-world events as elections and railway development. The refractive epigraphy I am arguing for here as constitutive of the novel is less lineally accretive than Miller's model. In *Middlemarch* we look through the epigraphs, as through a lens; and also back at the quoted text (as in a mirror), and both directions, one gesturing telescopically at the larger, the other condensing attention microscopically upon the former—and by

---

29 J. Hillis Miller, 'Optic and Semiotic in *Middlemarch*', in *The Worlds of Victorian Fiction*, ed. by Jerome Buckley (Cambridge: Harvard University Press, 1975), pp. 125–45 (126–27). For Miller, the optical is only one of three 'totalizing metaphors' that construe the novel, and is moreover subordinated in his reading to the more prominent 'textual' metaphors (fabric, web and so on) and metaphors of 'flow' or 'stream'. He also, in passing, suggests a meta-metaphor, describing these three as 'a family of intertwined metaphors and motifs' and glossing his own comment in a footnote: 'what, exactly, is the nature of the resemblance which binds together the members of this family and makes it seem of one genetic stock? Why, if Eliot's goal is to describe what is "really there," objectively, must there be more than one model in order to create a total picture?' Miller, 'Optic and Semiotic', p. 134. Like jesting Pilate he does not stay for an answer to these question.

extension, one inviting us to view the whole of this middled England as a vista or panorama, the other inviting us to zero-in on the minutiae that constitute this life-vista, as minutiae constitute all our lives. In all this Eliot is beautifully aware of the textuality of lived experience, not just in the sense that texts (like books and paintings) have a large role in creating and shaping us as human beings, but in the sense that life is a process of reading and re-reading other humans, and their situations, and life as such. In that, the radicalism of the epigraph is its insistence that such reading is always close-reading, actually; that the smallest of expressions or gestures may embody the largest of significances. The delicate sound of a flute resonates all the bell-like universe into contrapuntal music.

Towards the end, Ladislaw finds that he cannot pour out his heart to the (now widowed) Dorothea and that he is constrained to a brevity of expression. This, though, is presented in the novel as no bad thing.

> That simplicity of hers, holding up an ideal for others in her believing conception of them, was one of the great powers of her womanhood. And it had from the first acted strongly on Will Ladislaw. He felt, when he parted from her, that the brief words by which he had tried to convey to her his feeling about herself and the division which her fortune made between them, would only profit by their brevity when Dorothea had to interpret them: he felt that in her mind he had found his highest estimate.[30]

Brevity is the highest mode of communicating with the expansive simplicity of fulness—and vice versa: in a nutshell, it's the whole novel.

---

30   Eliot, *Middlemarch*, ch. 77.

Bibliography

Armstrong, Isobel, *Victorian Glassworlds: Glass Culture and the Imagination 1830–1880* (Oxford: Oxford University Press, 2008).

Baker, William, and Donald P Leinster-Mackay, *The Libraries of George Eliot and George Henry Lewes* (Victoria, BC: English Literary Studies, University of Victoria, 1981).

Baltazar, Lisa, 'The Critique of Anglican Biblical Scholarship in Eliot's "Middlemarch"', *Literature and Theology*, 15 (2001), 40–60, https://doi.org/10.1093/litthe/15.1.40

Bate, Walter Jackson, *The Burden of the Past and the English Poet* (London: Chatto and Windus, 1971).

Beale, Anthony, ed., *D. H. Lawrence: Selected Literary Criticism* (New York: Viking Press, 1956).

Beaty, Jerome, *Middlemarch from Notebook to Novel: A Study of George Eliot's Creative Method* (Illinois: University of Illinois Press, 1960).

Beaumont Francis, and John Fletcher, *The Maid's Tragedy* (1619), https://www.gutenberg.org/cache/epub/10847/pg10847.html

Beer, Gillian, *Darwin's Plots: Evolutionary Narrative in Darwin, George Eliot and Nineteenth-Century Fiction* (London: Routledge and Kegan Paul, 1983).

Béclard, Pierre Auguste, *Additions to the General Anatomy of Xavier Bichat*, trans. by George Hayward (Boston: Richardson and Lord, 1823).

'The Bell' [n.a.], *The Southern Review*, 22 (1877), 372.

Burrow, Colin, 'Who Wouldn't Buy It?', *London Review of Books*, 27.2 (2005), https://www.lrb.co.uk/the-paper/v27/n02/colin-burrow/who-wouldn-t-buy-it

Burton, Henry, *The Gospel According to St. Luke* (New York: A.C. Armstrong and Son, 1893).

Burstein, Miriam, *Narrating Women's History in Britain, 1770–1902* (Aldershot, Hampshire: Ashgate, 2004).

Cohen, J. Solis, *The Throat and the Voice* (London: Ward, Lock, & Co., 1880).

Dodd, Valerie, *George Eliot: an Intellectual Life* (London: Macmillan 1990)

Dryden, John, *The Hind and the Panther: A Poem, in Three Parts* (London: Printed for Jacob Tonson, 1687), http://www.online-literature.com/dryden/poetical-works-vol1/15/

Eagleton, Terry, *Sweet Violence: The Idea of the Tragic* (Oxford: Blackwell Publishers, 2003).

Eliot, George, *Adam Bede* (Edinburgh: William Blackwood and Sons, 1859), https://www.gutenberg.org/files/507/507-h/507-h.htm

Eliot, George, 'The Antigone and its Moral', *Leader*, 7 (March 29, 1856), 306.

Eliot, George, 'Art and Belles Lettres: Review of *Modern Painters*', *Westminster Review*, 65 (April 1856), 625–33.

Eliot, George, *Daniel Deronda* (Edinburgh: William Blackwood and Sons, 1876), http://www.gutenberg.org/files/7469/7469-h/7469-h.htm

Eliot, George, *Middlemarch* (Edinburgh: William Blackwood and Sons, 1871), http://www.gutenberg.org/files/145/145-h/145-h.htm

Eliot, George, *Mill on the Floss* (Edinburgh: William Blackwood, 1860), https://www.gutenberg.org/files/6688/6688-h/6688-h.htm

Empson, William, *Seven Types of Ambiguity*, rev. edn (New York: New Directions, 1947).

Erskine-Hill, Howard, 'Pope's Epigraphic Practice', *The Review of English Studies*, 62.254 (2011), 261–74, https://doi.org/10.1093/res/hgq027

Fleishman, Avrom, *George Eliot's Intellectual Life* (Cambridge: Cambridge University Press, 2010), https://doi.org/10.1017/cbo9780511691706

Flint, Kate, 'The Materiality of Middlemarch', in *Middlemarch in the Twenty-First Century*, ed. by Karen Chase (Oxford: Oxford University Press, 2006), pp. 65–86.

Fuller, Thomas, *The History of the Worthies of England* [1662], ed. by John Nichols (London: F.C. and J. Rivington, 1811).

Furst, Lilian R, 'Not So Long Ago: Historical Allusion in Realist Fiction' in *Through the Lens of the Reader: Explorations of European Narrative* (Albany: State University of New York Press, 1992), pp. 133–48.

Gaston, Sean, 'George Eliot and the Anglican Reader', *Literature and Theology*, 31.3 (2017), 318–37, https://doi.org/10.1093/litthe/frw026

Ginsburg, Michael Peled, 'Pseudonym, Epigraphs, and Narrative Voice: *Middlemarch* and the Problem of Authorship', *ELH*, 47.3 (1980), 542–58, https://doi.org/10.2307/2872795

Guizot, François-Pierre-Guillaume, *Cours D'Histoire Moderne: Histoire de la Civilisation en France* (Paris: Didier, 1846), vol. 3, https://www.google.co.uk/books/edition/Histoire_de_la_civilisation_en_France/_A-HYbpWLgQC?hl=en&gbpv=1

Guth, Deborah, 'George Eliot and Schiller: Narrative Ambivalence in *Middlemarch* and *Felix Holt*', *Modern Language Review*, 94.4 (1999), 913–24.

Guth, Deborah, *George Eliot and Schiller: Intertextuality and Cross-Cultural Discourse* (Surrey: Ashgate Publishing, 2003).

Handley, Graham, *George Eliot's Midlands: Passion in Exile* (London: Allison & Busby, 1991).

Herodotus, *The History of Herodotus*, trans. by Isaac Littlebury (Oxford: W. Baxter, 1824), p. 73, https://www.google.co.uk/books/edition/ The_History_of_Herodotus_Translated_By_I/XgPu0rLKGeIC?hl=en& gbpv=1

Higdon, David Leon, 'George Eliot and the Art of the Epigraph', *Nineteenth-Century Fiction*, 25.2 (1970), 127–51.

Homer, *Odyssey*, trans. by A. T. Murray (London: William Heinemann, 1919), https://www.perseus.tufts.edu/hopper/text?doc=Perseus%3Atext%3A199 9.01.0136%3Abook%3D5%3Acard%3D262

Horace, *The Art of Poetry: To the Pisos*, ed. and trans. by C. Smart and Theodore Alois Buckley (New York: Harper and Brothers, 1863), http://www.perseus. tufts.edu/hopper/text?doc=Perseus%3Atext%3A1999.02.0065%3Acard %3D1

Horowitz, Evan, 'Industrialism and the Victorian Novel'. Evan Horowitz, 'Industrialism and the Victorian Novel', in *The Oxford Handbook of the Victorian Novel*, ed. by Lisa Rodensky (Oxford: Oxford University Press, 2013), https:// www.oxfordhandbooks.com/view/10.1093/oxfordhb/9780199533145. 001.0001/oxfordhb-9780199533145-e-021373

'Hypocrisy' [n.a.], *The Saturday Review* [1869], in *The Living Age*, ed. by E. Littell (Boston: Littell and Gay, 1869), vol. 103, pp. 279–81, https://www.google.co.uk/ books/edition/Littell_s_Living_Age/uKBIAQAAMAAJ?hl=en&gbpv=1

Jackson, Catherine, 'The "Wonderful Properties of Glass": Liebig's Kaliapparat and the Practice of Chemistry in Glass', *Isis*, 106.1 (2015), 43–69, https://doi. org/10.1086/681036

Jameson, Fredric, *The Antimonies of Realism* (London: Verso Books, 2014).

Jones, H. S., *Intellect and Character in Victorian England: Mark Pattison and the Invention of the Don* (Cambridge: Cambridge University Press, 2007), https:// doi.org/10.1017/cbo9780511660283

Kidd, Colin, *The World of Mr Casaubon: Britain's Wars of Mythography 1700–1870* (Cambridge: Cambridge University Press, 2016), https://doi. org/10.1017/9781139226646

Kierkegaard, Søren, *On Authority and Revelation: The Book on Adler, or a Cycle of Ethico-Religious Essays*, trans. by Walter Lowrie (Princeton: Princeton University Press, 1955).

Kitchel, Anna Theresa, ed., *Quarry for Middlemarch* (Riverside: University of California Press, 1950).

Kuzmic, Tatiana, 'The German, the Sclave, and the Semite': Eastern Europe in the Imagination of George Eliot' *Nineteenth-Century Literature*, 68.4 (2014), 513–41, https://doi.org/10.1525/ncl.2014.68.4.513

Leckie, Barbara, *Open Houses: Poverty, the Novel, and the Architectural Idea in Nineteenth-Century Britain* (Philadelphia: University of Pennsylvania Press, 2018), https://doi.org/10.9783/9780812295177

Lewes, George Henry, *Aristotle: A Chapter from the History of Science* (London: Smith, Elder and Company, 1864).

Lewes, George Henry, *A Biographical History of Philosophy* (London: Charles Knight and Co., 1846).

Lewes, George Henry, *The Life and Works of Goethe* (London: David Nutt, 1855).

Lewes, George Henry, *The Life of Maximilien Robespierre: With Extracts from his Unpublished Correspondence* (Philadelphia: Carey and Hart, 1849).

Lewes, George Henry, 'Realism in Art: Recent German Fiction', *Westminster Review*, 70 (1858), 493–94.

Lucretius, *De Rerum Natura Libri Sex*, 2 vols, trans. by H. A. J. Munro (Cambridge: Deighton Bell & Co., 1866).

Macdonald, Fiona, 'The Only Surviving Recording of Virginia Woolf', *BBC Culture* (28 March 2016), https://www.bbc.com/culture/article/20160324-the-only-surviving-recording-of-virginia-woolf

Mars-Jones, Adam, 'Chop, Chop, Chop', *London Review of Books*, 38.2 (2016), https://www.lrb.co.uk/the-paper/v38/n02/adam-mars-jones/chop-chop-chop

Mason, Michael York, 'Middlemarch and Science: Problems of Life and Mind, *The Review of English Studies*, 22.86 (1971), 151–69, https://doi.org/10.1093/res/xxii.86.151

McClintock, John, *Cyclopaedia of Biblical, Theological, and Ecclesiastical Literature*, 2 vols (New York: Harper, 1868).

McDonagh, Josephine, 'The Early Novels', in *The Cambridge Companion to George Eliot*, ed. by George Levine (Cambridge: Cambridge University Press, 2001), pp. 38–56, https://doi.org/10.1017/ccol0521662672.003

McGann, Jerome J., *The Beauty of Inflections: Literary Investigations in Historical Method and Theory* (Oxford: Clarendon Press, 1985).

McKee, Patricia, *Heroic Commitment in Richardson, Eliot and James* (Princeton: Princeton University Press, 1986).

Miller, Frank E., *The Voice* (New York: G. Schirmer, 1910).

Miller, J. Hillis, 'Optic and Semiotic in *Middlemarch*', in *The Worlds of Victorian Fiction*, ed. by Jerome Buckley (Cambridge: Harvard University Press, 1975), pp. 125–45.

Miller, J. Hillis, *Reading for Our Time:* Adam Bede *and* Middlemarch *Revisited* (Edinburgh: Edinburgh University Press 2012).

Milton, Paul, 'Inheritance as the Key to all Mythologies: George Eliot and Legal Practice', *Mosaic: A Journal for the Interdisciplinary Study of Literature*, 28.1 (1995), 49–68.

Moldstad, David, '*The Mill on the Floss* and *Antigone*', *PMLA*, 85.3 (1970), 527–31, https://doi.org/10.2307/1261454

Moring, Meg M., 'George Eliot's Scrupulous Research: The Facts behind Eliot's Use of the Keepsake in *Middlemarch*', *Victorian Periodicals Review,* 26.1 (1993), 19–23.

Mudge, Isadore Gilbert, and Minnie Earl Sears, *A George Eliot Dictionary: The Characters and Scenes of the Novels, Stories, and Poems Alphabetically Arranged* (London: Routledge & Sons, 1924).

Müller, Karl Otfried, *History of the Literature of Ancient Greece, trans. by* George Cornewall Lewis (London: n.p., 1840).

Nuttall, A. D., *Dead from the Waist Down. Scholars and Scholarship in Literature and the Popular Imagination* (New Haven: Yale University Press, 2003).

Page, Norman (ed), *Tennyson: Interviews and Recollections* (London: Macmillan 1983)

Pascal, Blaise, *Pensées, introduction by T. S. Eliot (New York: E. P. Dutton and Co, 1958)*, https://www.gutenberg.org/files/18269/18269-h/18269-h.htm

Pattison, Mark, *Isaac Casaubon 1559–1614* (London: Longmans, Green and Co., 1875),

Phillips, Adam, 'Getting Ready to Exist', *London Review of Books*, 19.4 (1997), https://lrb.co.uk/the-paper/v19/n14/adam-phillips/getting-ready-to-exist

Phillips, Adam, *In Writing* (London: Penguin Books, 2019).

Polybius, *Histories*, ed. by Theodorus Büttner-Wobst after L. Dindorf (Leipzig: Teubner, 1893), http://www.perseus.tufts.edu/hopper/text?doc=Plb.+3.31 .&fromdoc=Perseus%3Atext%3A1999.01.0233

Purcell, Nicholas, '*Periploi*: Voyages around', *Oxford Classical Dictionary* (2015), https://oxfordre.com/classics/view/10.1093/acrefore/9780199381135. 001.0001/acrefore-9780199381135-e-4872

Rebellato, Dan, 'Sightlines: Foucault and Naturalist Theatre', in *Foucault's Theatres*, ed. by Tony Fisher and Kélina Gotman (Manchester: Manchester University Press, 2019), pp. 147–59, https://doi.org/10.7765/9781526132079.00020 Reynolds, Joseph William, *The Mystery of the Universe, Our Common Faith* (London: Kegan Paul, 1884).

Ricks, Christopher, *Allusion to the Poets* (Oxford: Oxford University Press, 2002).

Rignall, John, ed., *Oxford Reader's Companion to George Eliot* (Oxford: Oxford University Press, 2000).

Rothfield, Lawrence, *Vital Signs: Medical Realism in Nineteenth-Century Fiction* (Princeton: Princeton University Press, 1994).

Runcimann, David, *Political Hypocrisy: The Mask of Power, from Hobbes to Orwell and Beyond* (Princeton: Princeton University Press, 2010).

Ruskin, John, *Modern Painters*, vol. 5 (London: Smith, Elder and Co., 1860), https://www.gutenberg.org/files/44329/44329-h/44329-h.htm

Sanders, Andrew, *The Victorian Historical Novel 1840–1880* (London: Palgrave Macmillan, 1979)

Schiller, Friedrich, *Über naive und sentimentalische Dichtung* (1795–96), 'On Naïve and Sentimental Poetry', http://www.zeno.org/Literatur/M/Schiller,+Friedrich/

Scott, Walter, *The Antiquary* (Boston: Estes and Lauriat, 1893), https://www.gutenberg.org/files/7005/7005-h/7005-h.htm

Scott, Walter, *Guy Mannering, or the Astrologer* (Boston: Estes and Lauriat, 1893), https://www.gutenberg.org/files/5999/5999-h/5999-h.htm

Shaw, Harry E., *Narrating Reality: Austen, Scott, Eliot* (Ithaca: Cornell University Press, 1999).

Shuckburgh, Evelyn S., *The Histories of Polybius* (London: Macmillan and Co., 1889).

Shuttleworth, Sally, *George Eliot and Nineteenth-Century Science: The Make-Believe of a Beginning* (Cambridge: Cambridge University Press, 1984).

Tambling, Jeremy, '*Middlemarch*, Realism and the Birth of the Clinic', *ELH*, 57.4 (1990), 939–60.

Theocritis, 'Idyll XVI: The Graces; Or, Hiero', in *The Idylls of Theocritus, Bion and Moschus, and the War-songs of Tyrtaeus*, trans. by Rev. J. Banks (London: George Bell and Sons, 1878), p. 84.

Thomson, Patricia, 'The Three Georges', *Nineteenth-Century Fiction*, 18.2 (1963), 137–50, https://doi.org/10.1525/ncl.1963.18.2.99p0183d

Thonemann, Peter, 'Wall of Ice', *London Review of Books*, 30.7 (2008), 23–24.

Tolstoy, Leo, *Anna Karenina*, trans. by Constance Garnett (New York: Random House, 1939), https://www.gutenberg.org/files/1399/1399-h/1399-h.htm

Tomlinson, Charles, 'Mr Tomlinson's Experiments and Observations on Visible Vibration', *Records of General Science*, 2 (1835), 124–33.

Travis, Roger, 'From "Shattered Mummies" to "An Epic Life": Casaubon's Key to All Mythologies and Dorothea's Mythic Renewal in George Eliot's

Middlemarch', *International Journal of the Classical Tradition*, 5.3 (1999), 367–82, https://doi.org/10.1007/bf02687693

Vitaglione, Daniel, *George Eliot and George Sand: A Comparative Study* (unpublished PhD thesis, University of St Andrews, 1990), http://hdl.handle.net/10023/15069

Watt, Ian, *The Rise of the Novel: Studies in Defoe, Richardson and Fielding* (Berkeley: University of California Press 1957).

Watts, Alaric Alexander, ed., *The Literary Souvenir, or, Cabinet of Poetry and Romance* (London: [n.p.], 1826).

Webb, David, 'On Causality and Law in Lucretius and Contemporary Cosmology', in *Contemporary Encounters with Ancient Metaphysics*, ed. by Abraham Jacob Greenstine and Ryan J. Johnson (Edinburgh: Edinburgh University Press, 2017), pp. 254–69.

Wettlaufer, Alexandra K., 'George Sand, George Eliot, and the Politics of Difference', *The Romanic Review*, 107.1–4 (2016), 77–102, https://doi.org/10.1215/26885220-107.1-4.77

Williams, Raymond, *Keywords: A Vocabulary of Culture and Society* (Oxford: Oxford University Press, 1976).

Wood, James, 'Buckets of Empathy', *London Review of Books*, 22.7 (2000), https://www.lrb.co.uk/the-paper/v22/n07/james-wood/buckets-of-empathy

Wormald, Mark, 'Microscopy and Semiotic in *Middlemarch'*, *Nineteenth-Century Literature*, 50 (1996), 501–24, https://doi.org/10.2307/2933926

Wright, T. R., *"Middlemarch* as a Religious Novel, or Life without God', in *Images of Belief in Literature*, ed. by David Jasper (London: The Macmillan Press 1984), pp. 138–52.

Ziolkowski, Theodore J., 'The Craft(iness) of Epigraphs', *The Princeton University Library Chronicle*, 76.3 (2015), 519–20, https://doi.org/10.25290/prinunivlibrchro.76.3.0519

List of Illustrations

Index

About the Team

Alessandra Tosi was the managing editor for this book.

Adele Kreager performed the copy-editing and proofreading.

Anna Gatti designed the cover. The cover was produced in InDesign using the Fontin font.

Luca Baffa typeset the book in InDesign and produced the paperback and hardback editions. The text font is Tex Gyre Pagella; the heading font is Californian FB. Luca produced the EPUB, MOBI, PDF, HTML, and XML editions — the conversion is performed with open source software freely available on our GitHub page (https://github.com/OpenBookPublishers).

This book need not end here...

Share

All our books — including the one you have just read — are free to access online so that students, researchers and members of the public who can't afford a printed edition will have access to the same ideas. This title will be accessed online by hundreds of readers each month across the globe: why not share the link so that someone you know is one of them?

This book and additional content is available at:

https://doi.org/10.11647/OBP.0249

Customise

Personalise your copy of this book or design new books using OBP and third-party material. Take chapters or whole books from our published list and make a special edition, a new anthology or an illuminating coursepack. Each customised edition will be produced as a paperback and a downloadable PDF.

Find out more at:

https://www.openbookpublishers.com/section/59/1

You may also be interested in:

Jane Austen
Reflections of a Reader
By Nora Bartlett. Edited by Jane Stabler

https://doi.org/10.11647/OBP.0216

Love and its Critics
**From the Song of Songs to Shakespeare
and Milton's Eden**
By Michael Bryson and Arpi Movsesian

https://doi.org/10.11647/OBP.0117

Prose Fiction
An Introduction to the Semiotics of Narrative
By Ignasi Ribó

https://doi.org/10.11647/OBP.0187

www.ingramcontent.com/pod-product-compliance
Lightning Source LLC
Chambersburg PA
CBHW050348030726
47503CB00008B/2671